Rhoda Broughton

Tales for Christmas Eve

Rhoda Broughton

Tales for Christmas Eve

ISBN/EAN: 9783743317383

Manufactured in Europe, USA, Canada, Australia, Japa

Cover: Foto ©Andreas Hilbeck / pixelio.de

Manufactured and distributed by brebook publishing software
(www.brebook.com)

Rhoda Broughton

Tales for Christmas Eve

TALES FOR CHRISTMAS EVE.

TALES

FOR

CHRISTMAS EVE.

--

RHODA BROUGHTON,

AUTHOR OF

"COMETH UP AS A FLOWER,"

ETC., ETC.

LONDON:

RICHARD BENTLEY AND SON.

1873.

CONTENTS.

THE TRUTH, THE WHOLE TRUTH, AND NOTHING BUT THE TRUTH.

THE TRUTH, THE WHOLE TRUTH,

AND

NOTHING BUT THE TRUTH.

MRS. DE WYNT TO MRS. MONTRESOR.

"18, ECCLESTON SQUARE,

"*May 5th.*

"MY DEAREST CECILIA,

"TALK of the friendships of Orestes and Pylades, of Julie and Claire, what are they to ours? Did Pylades ever go *ventre à terre*, half over London on a day more broiling than any but an *âme damnée* could even imagine, in order that Orestes might be comfortably housed for the season? Did Claire ever hold sweet

1—2

experience, I arrived at about half-past five yesterday afternoon at 32, —— Street, May Fair.

" 'Failure No. 253, I don't doubt,' I said to myself, as I toiled up the steps with my soul athirst for afternoon tea, and feeling as ill-tempered as you please. So much for my spirit of prophecy. Fate, I have noticed, is often fond of contradicting us flat, and giving the lie to our little predictions. Once inside, I thought I had got into a small compartment of Heaven by mistake. Fresh as a daisy, clean as a cherry, bright as a seraph's face, it is all these, and a hundred more, only that my limited stock of similes is exhausted. Two drawing-rooms as pretty as ever woman crammed with people she did not care two straws about; white curtains with rose-coloured ones underneath, festooned in the sweetest way; marvellously, *immorally* becoming, my dear, as I ascertained entirely for your benefit, in the mirrors, of which there are about a dozen and a half; Persian mats, easy chairs, and lounges suited to every possible physical conformation, from the Apollo Belvedere to Miss Biffin; and a thousand of the important little trivialities that make up the sum of a woman's life : ormolu garden gates, handleless cups, naked boys and décolleté shepherdesses; not to speak of a family of china pugs, with blue ribbons round their necks, which ought of themselves to have added fifty pounds a year to the rent. Apropos, I asked, in fear and trembling, what the rent might be—'three hundred pounds a year.' A feather would have knocked me down. I could hardly believe my ears, and made the woman repeat it several times, that there might be no mistake. To this hour it is a mystery to me.

"With that suspiciousness which is so characteristic of you, you will immediately begin to hint that there must be some terrible unaccountable smell, or some odious inexplicable noise haunting the reception rooms. Nothing of the kind, the woman assured me, and she did not look as if she were telling stories. You will next suggest—remembering the rose-coloured curtains—that its last occupant was a member of the demi-monde. Wrong again. Its last occupant was an elderly and unexceptionable Indian officer, without a liver, and with a most lawful wife. They did not stay long, it is true, but then, as the housekeeper told me, he was a deplorable old hypochondriac, who never could bear to stay a fortnight in any one place. So lay aside that scepticism, which is your besetting sin, and give unfeigned thanks to St. Brigitta, or St. Gengulpha, or St. Catherine of Sienna, or whoever is your tutelar saint, for having provided you with a palace at the cost of a hovel, and for having sent you such an invaluable friend as

"Your attached

"ELIZABETH DE WYNT."

"P.S.—I am so sorry I shall not be in town to witness your first raptures, but dear Artie looks so pale and thin and tall after the hooping-cough, that I am sending him off at once to the sea, and as I cannot bear the child out of my sight, I am going into banishment likewise."

MRS. MONTRESOR TO MRS. DE WYNT.

"32, —— STREET, MAY FAIR,

"*May* 14*th.*

"DEAREST BESSY,

"WHY did not dear little Artie defer his
hooping-cough convalescence, &c., till August ?
It is very odd, to me, the perverse way in
which children always fix upon the most in-
convenient times and seasons for their diseases.
Here we are installed in our Paradise, and
have searched high and low, in every hole
and corner, for the serpent, without succeeding
in catching a glimpse of his spotted tail. Most
things in this world are disappointing, but 32,
—— Street, May Fair, is not. The mystery of
the rent is still a mystery. I have been for my

first ride in the row this morning : my horse
was a little fidgety ; I am half afraid that my
nerve is not what it was. I saw heaps of people I knew. Do you recollect Florence Watson?
What a wealth of red hair she had last year !
Well, that same wealth is black as the raven's
wing this year ! I wonder how people can
make such walking impositions of themselves,
don't you ? Adela comes to us next week ; I
am so glad. It is dull driving by oneself of an
afternoon ; and I always think that one young
woman alone in a brougham, or with only a
dog beside her, does not look *good*. We sent
round our cards a fortnight before we came up,
and have been already deluged with callers.
Considering that we have been two years
exiled from civilized life, and that London
memories are not generally of the longest, we
shall do pretty well, I think. Ralph Gordon
came to see me on Sunday; he is in the ——th
Hussars now. He has grown up such a *dear*

fellow, and *so* good-looking! Just my style, large and fair and whiskerless! Most men nowadays make themselves as like monkeys, or Scotch terriers, as they possibly can. I intend to be quite a *mother* to him. Dresses are gored to as *indecent* an extent as ever; short skirts are rampant. I am so sorry; I hate them. They make tall women look *lank*, and short ones insignificant. A knock! Peace is a word that might as well be expunged from one's London dictionary.

"Yours affectionately,

"CECILIA MONTRESOR."

MRS. DE WYNT TO MRS. MONTRESOR.

"THE LORD WARDEN, DOVER,

"*May* 18*th*.

" DEAREST CECILIA,

"YOU will perceive that I am about to
devote only one small sheet of note-paper to
you. This is from no dearth of time, Heaven
knows! time is a drug in the market here,
but from a total dearth of ideas. Any ideas
that I ever have, come to me from without,
from external objects; I am not clever enough
to generate any within myself. My life here is
not an eminently suggestive one. It is spent
in digging with a wooden spade, and eating
prawns. Those are my employments, at least;
my relaxation is going down to the Pier, to see

the Calais boat come in. When one is miserable oneself, it is decidedly consolatory to see some one more miserable still; and wretched and bored, and reluctant vegetable as I am, I am not *sea-sick.* I always feel my spirits rise after having seen that peevish, draggled procession of blue, green and yellow fellow-Christians file past me. There is a wind here *always*, in comparison of which the wind that behaved so violently to the corners of Job's house was a mere zephyr. There are heights to climb which require more daring perseverance than ever Wolfe displayed, with his paltry heights of Abraham. There are glaring white houses, glaring white roads, glaring white cliffs. If any one knew how unpatriotically I detest the chalk-cliffs of Albion! Having grumbled through my two little pages —I have actually been reduced to writing very large in order to fill even them—I will send off my dreary little billet. How I wish I could get into the envelope myself too, and whirl up with it to dear, beautiful, filthy London. Not more heavily could Madame de Staël have sighed for Paris from among the shades of Coppet.

"Your disconsolate

BESSY."

MRS. MONTRESOR TO MRS. DE WYNT.

"32, —— STREET, MAY FAIR,

"*May 27th.*

"OH, my dearest Bessy, how I wish we were out of this dreadful, dreadful house! Please don't think me very ungrateful for saying this, after your taking such pains to provide us with a Heaven upon earth, as you thought.

"What has happened could, of course, have been neither foretold, nor guarded against, by any human being. About ten days ago, Benson (my maid) came to me with a very long face, and said, 'If you please, 'm, did you know that this house was *haunted?*' I was *so* startled: you know what a coward I am. I

said, 'Good Heavens! No! is it?' 'Well,
'm, I'm pretty nigh sure it is,' she said, and
the expression of her countenance was about
as lively as an undertaker's; and then she
told me that cook had been that morning to
order in groceries from a shop in the neigh-
bourhood, and on her giving the man the
direction where to send the things to, he had
said, with a very peculiar smile, 'No. 32, ——
Street, eh?·h'm? I wonder how long *you'll*
stand it; last lot held out just a fortnight.'
He looked so odd that she asked him what he
meant, but he only said, 'Oh! nothing; only
that parties never *did* stay long at 32. He
had known parties go in one day, and out the
next, and during the last four years he had
never known any remain over the month.'
Feeling a good deal alarmed by this information, she naturally inquired the reason; but
he declined to give it, saying that if she had
not found it out for herself, she had much

better leave it alone, as it would only frighten her out of her wits; and on her insisting and urging him, she could only extract from him, that the house had such a villanously bad name, that the owners were glad to let it for a mere song. You know how firmly I believe in apparitions, and what an unutterable fear I have of them; anything material, tangible, that I can lay hold of—anything of the same fibre, blood, and bone as myself, I could, I think, confront bravely enough; but the mere thought of being brought face to face with the 'bodiless dead,' makes my brain unsteady. The moment Henry came in, I ran to him, and told him; but he pooh-poohed the whole story, laughed at me, and asked whether we should turn out of the prettiest house in London, at the very height of the season, because a grocer said it had a bad name. Most good things that had ever been in the world had had a bad name in their day; and,

2

moreover, the man had probably a motive for
taking away the house's character, some
friend for whom he coveted the charming
situation and the low rent. He derided my
' babyish fears,' as he called them, to such an
extent that I felt half ashamed, and yet not
quite comfortable, either; and then came the
usual rush of London engagements, during
which one has no time to think of anything
but how to speak, and act, and look for the
moment then present. Adela was to arrive
yesterday, and in the morning our weekly
hamper of flowers, fruit, and vegetables
arrived from home. I always dress the flower-
vases myself, servants are so tasteless; and as
I was arranging them, it occurred to me—you
know Adela's passion for flowers—to carry
up one particular cornucopia of roses and
mignonette and set it on her toilet-table, as a
pleasant surprise for her. As I came downstairs, I had seen the housemaid—a fresh,

round-faced country girl—go into the room, which was being prepared for Adela, with a pair of sheets that she had been airing over her arm. I went upstairs very slowly, as my cornucopia was full of water, and I was afraid of spilling some. I turned the handle of the bedroom-door and entered, keeping my eyes fixed on my flowers, to see how they bore the transit, and whether any of them had fallen out. Suddenly a sort of shiver passed over me; and feeling frightened—I did not know why—I looked up quickly. The girl was standing by the bed, leaning forward a little with her hands clenched in each other, rigid, every nerve tense; her eyes, wide open, starting out of her head, and a look of unutterable stony horror in them; her cheeks and mouth not pale, but livid as those of one that died awhile ago in mortal pain. As I looked at her, her lips moved a little, and an awful hoarse voice, not like hers in the least, said,

'Oh! my God, I have seen it!' and then she
fell down suddenly, like a log, with a heavy
noise. Hearing the noise, loudly audible all
through the thin walls and floors of a London
house, Benson came running in, and between
us we managed to lift her on to the bed, and
tried to bring her to herself by rubbing her
feet and hands, and holding strong salts to her
nostrils. And all the while we kept glancing
over our shoulders, in a vague cold terror of
seeing some awful, shapeless apparition. Two
long hours she lay in a state of utter uncon-
sciousness. Meanwhile Harry, who had been
down to his club, returned. At the end of the
two hours we succeeded in bringing her back
to sensation and life, but only to make the
awful discovery that she was raving mad.
She became so violent that it required all the
combined strength of Harry and Phillips (our
butler) to hold her down in the bed. Of
course, we sent off instantly for a doctor, who,

on her growing a little calmer towards evening, removed her in a cab to his own house. He has just been here to tell me that she is now pretty quiet, not from any return to sanity, but from sheer exhaustion. We are, of course, utterly in the dark as to *what* she saw, and her ravings are far too disconnected and unintelligible to afford us the slightest clue. I feel so completely shattered and upset by this awful occurrence, that you will excuse me, dear, I'm sure, if I write incoherently. One thing, I need hardly tell you, and that is, that no earthly consideration would induce me to allow Adela to occupy that terrible room. I shudder and run by quickly as I pass the door.

"Yours, in great agitation,

"CECILIA."

MRS. DE WYNT TO MRS. MONTRESOR.

"THE LORD WARDEN, DOVER,
"*May* 28*th*.

" DEAREST CECILIA,

" YOURS just come ; how very dreadful !
But I am still unconvinced as to the house
being in fault. You know I feel a sort of
godmother to it, and responsible for its good
behaviour. Don't you think that what the
girl had might have been a fit ? Why not ?
I myself have a cousin who is subject to
seizures of the kind, and immediately on
being attacked his whole body becomes rigid,
his eyes glassy and staring, his complexion
livid, exactly as in the case you describe. Or,
if not a fit, are you sure that she has not

been subject to fits of madness? *Please* be sure and ascertain whether there is not insanity in her family. It is so common now-a-days, and so much on the increase, that nothing is more likely. You know my utter disbelief in ghosts. I am convinced that most of them, if run to earth, would turn out about as genuine as the famed Cock Lane one. But even allowing the possibility, nay, the actual unquestioned existence of ghosts in the abstract, is it likely that there should be anything to be seen so horribly fear-inspiring, as to send a perfectly sane person *in one instant* raving mad, which you, after three weeks' residence in the house, have never caught a glimpse of? According to your hypothesis, your whole household ought, by this time, to be stark, staring mad. Let me implore you not to give way to a panic which may, possibly, probably prove utterly ground-less. Oh, how I wish I were with you, to make you listen to reason! Artie ought to be the best prop ever woman's old age was furnished with, to indemnify me for all he and his hooping-cough have made me suffer. Write immediately, please, and tell me how the poor patient progresses. Oh, had I the wings of a dove! I shall be on wires till I hear again.

"Yours,

"BESSY."

MRS. MONTRESOR TO MRS. DE WYNT.

"No. 5, Bolton Street, Piccadilly,
"*June 12th.*

"Dearest Bessy,

"You will see that we have left that terrible, hateful, fatal house. How I wish we had escaped from it sooner! Oh, my dear Bessy, I shall never be the same woman again if I live to be a hundred. Let me try to be coherent, and to tell you connectedly what has happened. And first, as to the house-maid, she has been removed to a lunatic asylum, where she remains in much the same state. She has had several lucid intervals, and during them has been closely, pressingly questioned as to what it was she saw;

but she has maintained an absolute, hopeless silence, and only shudders, moans, and hides her face in her hands when the subject is broached. Three days ago I went to see her, and on my return was sitting resting in the drawing-room, before going to dress for dinner, talking to Adela about my visit, when Ralph Gordon walked in. He has always been walking in the last ten days, and Adela has always flushed up and looked happy, poor little cat, whenever he made his appearance. He looked very handsome, dear fellow, just come in from the park in a coat that fitted like a second skin, lavender gloves, and a gardenia. He seemed in tremendous spirits, and was as sceptical as even you could be, as to the ghostly origin of Sarah's seizure. 'Let me come here to-night and sleep in that room; *do*, Mrs. Montresor,' he said, looking very eager and excited, 'with the gas lit and a poker, I'll engage to exorcise every demon

that shows his ugly nose; even if I should
find—

> "'Seven white ghostisses
> Sitting on seven white postisses.'

"'You don't mean really?' I asked, incredulously. 'Don't I? that's all,' he answered
emphatically. 'I should like nothing better.
Well, is it a bargain?' Adela turned quite
pale. 'Oh, don't,' she said, hurriedly, '*please*,
don't; why should you run such a risk?
How do you know that you might not be
sent mad too?' He laughed very heartily,
and coloured a little with pleasure at seeing
the interest she took in his safety. 'Never
fear,' he said, 'it would take more than a
whole squadron of departed ones, with the
old gentleman at their head, to send me
crazy.' He was so eager, so persistent, so
thoroughly in earnest, that I yielded at last,
though with a certain strong reluctance,

to his entreaties. Adela's blue eyes filled
with tears, and she walked away hastily to
the conservatory, and stood picking bits of
heliotrope to hide them. Nevertheless, Ralph
got his own way; it was so difficult to refuse
him anything. We gave up all our engagements for the evening, and he did the same
with his. At about ten o'clock he arrived,
accompanied by a friend and brother officer,
Captain Burton, who was anxious to see the
result of the experiment. 'Let me go up at
once,' he said, looking very happy and ani-
mated. 'I don't know when I have felt in
such good tune; a new sensation is a luxury
not to be had every day of one's life; turn
the gas up as high as it will go; provide a
good stout poker, and leave the issue to Pro-
vidence and me.' We did as he bid. 'It's all
ready now,' Henry said, coming downstairs
after having obeyed his orders; 'the room is
nearly as light as day. Well, good luck to

you, old fellow !' 'Good-bye, Miss Bruce,' Ralph said, going over to Adela, and taking her hand with a look, half laughing, half sentimental—

> " 'Fare thee well, and if for ever,
> Then for ever, fare thee well,'

that is my last dying speech and confession. Now mind,' he went on, standing by the table, and addressing us all ; 'if I ring once, *don't* come. I may be flurried, and lay hold of the bell without thinking ; if I ring twice, *come.*' Then he went, jumping up the stairs three steps at a time, and humming a tune. As for us, we sat in different attitudes of expectation and listening about the drawing-room. At first we tried to talk a little, but it would not do ; our whole souls seemed to have passed into our ears. The clock's ticking sounded as loud as a great church bell close to one's ear. Addy lay on the sofa, with her dear little white face hidden in the cushions. So we sat for exactly an hour; but it seemed like two years, and just as the clock began to strike eleven, a sharp ting, ting, ting, rang clear and shrill through the house. 'Let us go,' said Addy, starting up and running to the door. 'Let us go,' I cried too, following her. But Captain Burton stood in the way, and intercepted our progress. 'No,' he said, decisively, 'you must not go; remember Gordon told us distinctly, if he rang once *not* to come. I know the sort of fellow he is, and that nothing would annoy him more than having his directions disregarded.'

"'Oh, nonsense!' Addy cried, passionately, 'he would never have rung if he had not seen something dreadful; do, *do* let us go!' she ended, clasping her hands. But she was overruled, and we all went back to our seats. Ten minutes more of suspense, next door to unendurable, I felt a lump in my throat, a gasping for breath;—ten minutes on the clock, but a thousand centuries on our hearts. Then again, loud, sudden, violent the bell rang! We made a simultaneous rush to the door. I don't think we were one second flying upstairs. Addy was first. Almost simultaneously she and I burst into the room. There he was, standing in the middle of the floor, rigid, petrified, with that same look— that look that is burnt into my heart in letters of fire—of awful, unspeakable, stony fear on his brave young face. For one instant he stood thus; then stretching out his arms stiffly before him, he groaned in a terrible, husky voice, 'Oh, my God; I have seen it!' and fell down *dead.* Yes, *dead.* Not in a swoon or in a fit, but *dead.* Vainly we tried to bring back the life to that strong young heart; it will never come back again till that day when the earth and the sea give up the dead that are therein. I cannot see the page for the tears that are blinding me; he was such a dear fellow! I can't write any more to-day.

           " Your broken-hearted

                " CECILIA."

This is a true story.

THE MAN WITH THE NOSE.

THE MAN WITH THE NOSE.

[The details of this little story are of course imaginary, but the main incidents are, to the best of my belief, facts. They happened twenty, or more than twenty years ago.]

CHAPTER I.

"LET us get a map and see what places look pleasantest?" says she.

"As for that," reply I, "on a map most places look equally pleasant."

"Never mind ; get one !"

I obey.

"Do you like the seaside?" asks Elizabeth, lifting her little brown head and her small happy white face from the English sea-coast along which her forefinger is slowly travelling.

"Since you ask me, distinctly *no*," reply I, for once venturing to have a decided opinion of my own, which during the last few weeks of imbecility I can be hardly said to have had. "I broke my last wooden spade five and twenty years ago. I have but a poor opinion of cockles—sandy red-nosed things, are not they? and the air always makes me bilious."

"Then we certainly will not go there," says Elizabeth, laughing. "A bilious bridegroom! alliterative but horrible! None of our friends show the least eagerness to lend us their country house."

"Oh that God would put it into the hearts of men to take their wives straight home, as their fathers did," say I, with a cross groan.

"It is evident, therefore, that we must go somewhere," returns she, not heeding the aspiration contained in my last speech, making her

forefinger resume its employment, and reaching Torquay.

"I suppose so," say I, with a sort of sigh;
"for once in our lives we must resign ourselves to having the finger of derision pointed
at us by waiters and landlords."

"You shall leave your new portmanteau at
home, and I will leave all my best clothes, and
nobody will guess that we are bride and
bridegroom; they will think that we have
been married—oh, ever since the world began"
(opening her eyes very wide).

I shake my head. "With an old portmanteau and in rags we shall still have the mark
of the beast upon us."

"Do you mind much? do you hate being
ridiculous?" asks Elizabeth, meekly, rather
depressed by my view of the case; "because if
so, let us go somewhere out of the way,
where there will be very few people to laugh
at us."

"On the contrary," return I, stoutly, "we will betake ourselves to some spot where such as we do chiefly congregate—where we shall be swallowed up and lost in the multitude of our fellow-sinners." A pause devoted to reflection. "What do you say to Killarney?" say I, cheerfully.

"There are a great many fleas there, I believe," replies Elizabeth, slowly; "flea-bites make large lumps on me; you would not like me if I were covered with large lumps."

At the hideous ideal picture thus presented to me by my little beloved I relapse into inarticulate idiocy; emerging from which by-and-by, I suggest "The Lakes?" My arm is round her, and I feel her supple body shiver though it is mid July, and the bees are booming about in the still and sleepy noon garden outside.

"Oh—no—no—not *there !*"

"Why such emphasis?" I ask gaily; "more fleas? At this rate, and with this *sine quâ non*, our choice will grow limited."

"Something dreadful happened to me there," she says, with another shudder. "But indeed I did not think there was any harm in it—I never thought anything would come of it."

"What the devil was it?" cry I, in a jealous heat and hurry; "what the mischief *did* you do, and why have not you told me about it before?"

"I did not *do* much," she answers meekly, seeking for my hand, and when found kissing it in timid deprecation of my wrath; "but I was ill—very ill—there; I had a nervous fever. I was in a bed hung with a chintz with a red and green fern-leaf pattern on it. I have always hated red and green fern-leaf chintzes ever since."

"It would be possible to avoid the obnoxious bed, would not it?" say I, laughing a little. "Where does it lie? Windermere? Ulleswater? Wastwater? Where?"

"We were at Ulleswater," she says, speaking rapidly, while a hot colour grows on her small white cheeks—"Papa, mamma, and I; and there came a mesmeriser to Penrith, and we went to see him—everybody did—and he asked leave to mesmerise me—he said I should be such a good medium—and—and—I did not know what it was like. I thought it would be quite good fun—and—and—I let him."

She is trembling exceedingly; even the loving pressure of my arms cannot abate her shivering.

"Well?"

"And after that I do not remember anything—I believe I did all sorts of extraordinary things that he told me—sang and danced, and made a fool of myself—but when I came

home I was very ill, very—I lay in bed for
five whole weeks, and—and was off my head,
and said odd and wicked things that you
would not have expected me to say—that
dreadful bed! shall I ever forget it?"

"We will *not* go to the Lakes," I say,
decisively, "and we will not talk any more
about mesmerism."

"That is right," she says, with a sigh of
relief, "I try to think about it as little as
possible; but sometimes, in the dead black of
the night, when God seems a long way off, and
the devil near, it comes back to me so strongly
—I feel, do not you know, as if he were *there*
—somewhere in the room, and I *must* get up
and follow him."

"Why should not we go abroad?" suggest
I, abruptly turning the conversation.

"Why, indeed?" cries Elizabeth, recovering
her gaiety, while her pretty blue eyes begin to
dance. "How stupid of us not to have thought

of it before; only *abroad* is a big word. *What* abroad ?"

"We must be content with something short of Central Africa," I say, gravely, "as I think our one hundred and fifty pounds would hardly take us that far."

"Wherever we go, we must buy a dialogue book," suggests my little bride elect, "and I will learn some phrases before we start."

"As for that, the Anglo-Saxon tongue takes one pretty well round the world," reply I, with a feeling of complacent British swagger, putting my hands in my breeches pockets.

"Do you fancy the Rhine ?" says Elizabeth, with a rather timid suggestion; "I know it is the fashion to run it down nowadays, and call it a cocktail river; but—but—after all it cannot be so *very* contemptible, or Byron could not have said such noble things about it."

" The castled crag of Drachenfels
  Frowns o'er the wide and winding Rhine,
  Whose breast of waters broadly swells
  Between the banks which bear the vine,"

say I, spouting. " After all, that proves
nothing, for Byron could have made a silk
purse out of a sow's ear."

" The Rhine will not do then ?" says she,
resignedly, suppressing a sigh.

" On the contrary, it will do admirably : it
is a cocktail river, and I do not care who
says it is not," reply I, with illiberal positive-
ness ; " but everybody should be able to say
so from their own experience, and not from
hearsay : the Rhine let it be, by all means."

So the Rhine it is.

CHAPTER II.

I HAVE got over it; we have both got over
it tolerably, creditably; but after all, it is a
much severer ordeal for a man than a woman,
who, with a bouquet to occupy her hands,
and a veil to gently shroud her features, need
merely be prettily passive. I am alluding, I
need hardly say, to the religious ceremony of
marriage, which I flatter myself I have gone
through with a stiff sheepishness not un-
worthy of my country. It is a three-days-old
event now, and we are getting used to belong-
ing to one another, though Elizabeth still takes
off her ring twenty times a day to admire its

bright thickness ; still laughs when she hears
herself called "Madame." Three days ago,
we kissed all our friends, and left them to
make themselves ill on our cake, and criticise
our bridal behaviour, and now we are at
Brussels, she and I, feeling oddly, joyfully free
from any chaperone. We have been mildly
sight-seeing—very mildly, most people would
say, but we have resolved not to take our
pleasure with the railway speed of Americans,
or the hasty sadness of our fellow Britons.
Slowly and gaily we have been taking ours.
To-day we have been to visit Wiertz's pic-
tures. Have you ever seen them, oh reader ?
They are known to comparatively few people,
but if you have a taste for the unearthly
terrible—if you wish to sup full of horrors,
hasten thither. We have been peering
through the appointed peep-hole at the
horrible cholera picture—the man buried alive
by mistake, pushing up the lid of his coffin,

and stretching a ghastly face and livid hands
out of his winding sheet towards you, while
awful grey-blue coffins are piled around, and
noisome toads and giant spiders crawl damply
about. On first seeing it, I have reproached
myself for bringing one of so nervous a tem-
perament as Elizabeth to see so haunting and
hideous a spectacle; but she is less impressed
than I expected—less impressed than I myself
am.

"He is very lucky to be able to get his
lid up," she says, with a half-laugh; "we
should find it hard work to burst our brass
nails, should not we? When you bury me,
dear, fasten me down very slightly, in case
there may be some mistake."

And now all the long and quiet July
evening we have been prowling together
about the streets. Brussels is the town of
towns for *flâner*-ing—have been flattening
our noses against the shop windows, and

making each other imaginary presents. Elizabeth has not confined herself to imagination, however; she has made me buy her a little bonnet with feathers—"in order to look married," as she says, and the result is such a delicious picture of a child playing at being grown up, having practised a theft on its mother's wardrobe, that for the last two hours I have been in a foolish ecstasy of love and laughter over her and it. We are at the "Bellevue," and have a fine suite of rooms, *au premier*, evidently specially devoted to the English, to the gratification of whose well-known loyalty the Prince and Princess of Wales are simpering from the walls. Is there any one in the three kingdoms who knows his own face as well as he knows the faces of Albert Victor and Alexandra? The long evening has at last slidden into night—night far advanced—night melting into earliest day. All Brussels is asleep. One moment ago I

also was asleep, soundly as any log. What is
it that has made me take this sudden, head-
long plunge out of sleep into wakefulness?
Who is it that is clutching at and calling upon
me? What is it that is making me struggle
mistily up into a sitting posture, and try to
revive my sleep-numbed senses? A summer
night is never wholly dark; by the half light
that steals through the closed *persiennes* and
open windows I see my wife standing beside
my bed; the extremity of terror on her face,
and her fingers digging themselves with painful tenacity into my arm.

"Tighter, tighter!" she is crying, wildly.
"What are you thinking of? You are letting
me go!"

"Good heavens!" say I, rubbing my eyes,
while my muddy brain grows a trifle clearer.
"What is it? What has happened? Have
you had a nightmare?"

"You saw him," she says, with a sort of

sobbing breathlessness; "you know you did! You saw him as well as I."

"I!" cry I, incredulously—"not I. Till this second I have been fast asleep. *I* saw nothing."

"You did!" she cries, passionately. "You know you did. Why do you deny it? You were as frightened as I?"

"As I live," I answer, solemnly, "I know no more than the dead what you are talking about; till you woke me by calling me and catching hold of me, I was as sound asleep as the seven sleepers."

"Is it possible that it can have been a *dream?*" she says, with a long sigh, for a moment loosing my arm, and covering her face with her hands. "But no—in a dream I should have been somewhere else, but I was here—*here*—on that bed, and he stood *there*," pointing with her forefinger, "just *there*, between the foot of it and the window!"

She stops, panting.

"It is all that brute Wiertz," say I, in a fury. "I wish I had been buried alive myself, before I had been fool enough to take you to see his beastly daubs."

"Light a candle," she says, in the same breathless way, her teeth chattering with fright. "Let us make sure that he is not hidden somewhere in the room."

"How could he be ?" say I, striking a match ; "the door is locked."

"He might have got in by the balcony," she answers, still trembling violently.

"He would have had to have cut a very large hole in the *persiennes*," say I, half-mockingly. "See, they are intact and well fastened on the inside."

She sinks into an arm-chair, and pushes her loose soft hair from her white face.

"It *was* a dream then, I suppose ?"

She is silent for a moment or two, while I

bring her a glass of water, and throw a dressing-gown round her cold and shrinking form.

"Now tell me, my little one," I say, coaxingly, sitting down at her feet, "what it was —what you thought you saw?"

"*Thought* I saw!" echoes she, with indignant emphasis, sitting upright, while her eyes sparkle feverishly. "I am as certain that I saw him standing there as I am that I see that candle burning—that I see this chair—that I see you."

"*Him!* but who is *him?*"

She falls forward on my neck, and buries her face in my shoulder.

"That—dreadful—man!" she says, while her whole body is one tremor.

"*What* dreadful man?" cry I, impatiently.

She is silent.

"Who was he?"

"I do not know."

"Did you ever see him before?"

"Oh, no—no, never! I hope to God I may never see him again!"

"What was he like?"

"Come closer to me," she says, laying hold of my hand with her small and chilly fingers; "stay *quite* near me, and I will tell you,"—after a pause—"he had a *nose!*"

"My dear soul," cry I, bursting out with a loud laugh in the silence of the night, "do not most people have noses? Would not he have been much more dreadful if he had had *none?*"

"But it was *such* a nose!" she says, with perfect trembling gravity.

"A bottle nose?" suggest I, still cackling.

"For heaven's sake, don't laugh!" she says, nervously; "if you had seen his face, you would have been as little disposed to laugh as I."

"But his nose?" return I, suppressing my

merriment; "what kind of nose was it? See, I am as grave as a judge."

"It was very prominent," she answers, in a sort of awe-struck half-whisper, "and very sharply chiselled; the nostrils very much cut out." A little pause. "His eyebrows were one straight black line across his face, and under them his eyes burnt like dull coals of fire, that shone and yet did not shine; they looked like dead eyes, sunken, half extinguished, and yet sinister."

"And what did he do?" ask I, impressed, despite myself, by her passionate earnestness; "when did you first see him?"

"I was asleep," she said—"at least I thought so—and suddenly I opened my eyes, and he was *there—there*"—pointing again with trembling finger—"between the window and the bed."

"What was he doing? Was he walking about?"

"He was standing as still as stone—I never saw any live thing so still—*looking* at me; he never called or beckoned, or moved a finger, but his eyes *commanded* me to come to him, as the eyes of the mesmeriser at Penrith did." She stops, breathing heavily. I can hear her heart's loud and rapid beats.

"And you?" I say, pressing her more closely to my side, and smoothing her troubled hair.

"I *hated* it," she cries, excitedly; "I loathed it—abhorred it. I was ice-cold with fear and horror, but—I *felt* myself going to him."

"Yes?"

"And then I shrieked out to you, and you came running, and caught fast hold of me, and held me tight at first—quite tight—but presently I felt your hold slacken—slacken— and though I *longed* to stay with you, though I was *mad* with fright, yet I felt myself pulling strongly away from you—going to him;

and he—he stood there always looking—looking—and then I gave one last loud shriek, and I suppose I awoke—and it was a dream !"

" I never heard of a clearer case of nightmare," say I, stoutly; "that vile Wiertz ! I should like to see his whole *Musée* burnt by the hands of the hangman to-morrow."

She shakes her head. "It had nothing to say to Wiertz; what it meant I do not know, but——"

" It meant nothing," I answer, reassuringly, " except that for the future we will go and see none but good and pleasant sights, and steer clear of charnel-house fancies."

CHAPTER III.

ELIZABETH is now in a position to decide
whether the Rhine is a cocktail river or no,
for she is on it, and so am I.   We are sitting,
with an awning over our heads, and little
wooden stools under our feet.   Elizabeth has
a small sailor's hat and blue ribbon on her
head.   The river breeze has blown it rather
awry ; has tangled her plenteous hair ; has
made a faint pink stain on her pale cheeks.
It is some fête day, and the boat is crowded.
Tables, countless camp-stools, volumes of black
smoke pouring from the funnel, as we steam
along.   " Nothing to the Caledonian Canal !"

cries a burly Scotchman in leggings, speaking with loud authority, and surveying with an air of contempt the eternal vine-clad slopes, that sound so well, and look so *sticky* in reality. " Cannot hold a candle to it !" A rival bride and bridegroom opposite, sitting together like love-birds under an umbrella, looking into each other's eyes instead of at the Rhine scenery.

" They might as well have stayed at home, might not they ?" says my wife, with a little air of superiority. " Come, we are not so bad as that, are we ?"

A storm comes on : hailstones beat slantwise and reach us—stone and sting us right under our awning. Everybody rushes down below, and takes the opportunity to feed ravenously. There are few actions more disgusting than eating *can* be made. A handsome girl close to us—her immaturity evidenced by the two long tails of black hair

down her back—is thrusting her knife half
way down her throat.

" Come on deck again," says Elizabeth, disgusted and frightened at this last sight. " The
hail was much better than this !"

So we return to our camp-stools, and sit
alone under one mackintosh in the lashing
storm, with happy hearts and empty stomachs.

" Is not this better than any luncheon ?"
asks Elizabeth, triumphantly, while the rain-
drops hang on her long and curled lashes.

" Infinitely better," reply I, madly struggling with the umbrella to prevent its being
blown inside out, and gallantly ignoring a
species of gnawing sensation at my entrails.

The squall clears off by and by, and we go
steaming, steaming on past the unnumbered
little villages by the water's edge with church
spires and pointed roof, past the countless
rocks with their little pert castles perched on
the top of them, past the tall, stiff poplar

rows. The church bells are ringing gaily as we go by. A nightingale is singing from a wood. The black eagle of Prussia droops on the stream behind us, swish-swish through the dull green water. A fat woman who is interested in it, leans over the back of the boat, and by some happy effect of crinoline, displays to her fellow-passengers two yards of thick white cotton legs. She is, fortunately for herself, unconscious of her generosity.

The day steals on; at every stopping place more people come on. There is hardly elbow room; and, what is worse, almost everybody is drunk. Rocks, castles, villages, poplars, slide by, while the paddles churn always the water, and the evening draws greyly on. At Bingen a party of big blue Prussian soldiers, very drunk, "glorious" as Tam o' Shanter, come and establish themselves close to us. They call for Lager Beer; talk at the tip-top of their strong voices; two of them begin to

spar ; all seem inclined to sing. Elizabeth is
frightened. We are two hours late in arriving
at Biebrich. It is half an hour more before
we can get ourselves and our luggage into a
carriage and set off along the winding road to
Wiesbaden. "The night is chilly, but not
dark." There is only a little shabby bit of a
moon, but it shines as hard as it can. Elizabeth is quite worn out, her tired head droops
in uneasy sleep on my shoulder. Once she
wakes up with a start.

"Are you sure that it meant nothing ?" she
asks, looking me eagerly in my face; "do
people often have such dreams ?"

"Often, often," I answer, reassuringly.

"I am always afraid of falling asleep now,"
she says, trying to sit upright and keep her
heavy eyes open, "for fear of seeing him
standing there again. Tell me, do you think
I shall ? Is there any chance, any probability
of it ?"

"None, none!"

We reach Wiesbaden at last, and drive up to the Hôtel des Quatre Saisons. By this time it is full midnight. Two or three men are standing about the door. Morris, the maid, has got out—so have I, and I am holding out my hand to Elizabeth, when I hear her give one piercing scream, and see her with ash-white face and starting eyes point with her fore-finger——

"There he is!—there!—there!"

I look in the direction indicated, and just catch a glimpse of a tall figure, standing half in the shadow of the night, half in the gas-light from the hotel. I have not time for more than one cursory glance, as I am interrupted by a cry from the bystanders, and turning quickly round, am just in time to catch my wife, who falls in utter insensibility into my arms. We carry her into a room on the ground floor; it is small, noisy, and hot, but it is the nearest at hand. In about an hour she re-opens her eyes. A strong shudder makes her quiver from head to foot.

"Where is he?" she says, in a terrified whisper, as her senses come slowly back. "He is somewhere about—somewhere near. I feel that he is!"

"My dearest child, there is no one here but Morris and me," I answer, soothingly. "Look for yourself. See."

I take one of the candles and light up each corner of the room in succession.

"You saw him!" she says, in trembling hurry, sitting up and clenching her hands together. "I know you did—I pointed him out to you—you *cannot* say that it was a dream *this* time."

"I saw two or three ordinary looking men as we drove up," I answer, in a commonplace, matter-of-fact tone. "I did not notice anything remarkable about any of them; you know the fact is, darling, that you have had nothing to eat all day, nothing but a biscuit, and you are over-wrought, and fancy things."

"Fancy!" echoes she, with strong irritation. "How you talk! Was I ever one to fancy things? I tell you that as sure as I sit here —as sure as you stand there—I saw him— *him*—the man I saw in my dream, if it was a dream. There was not a hair's breadth of difference between them—and he was looking at me—looking——"

She breaks off into hysterical sobbing.

"My dear child!" say I, thoroughly alarmed, and yet half angry, "for God's sake do not work yourself up into a fever: wait till to-morrow, and we will find out who he is, and all about him; you yourself will laugh when we discover that he is some harmless bag-man."

"Why not *now?*" she says, nervously;

"why cannot you find out *now — this minute ?*"

"Impossible ! Everybody is in bed ! Wait till to-morrow, and all will be cleared up."

The morrow comes, and I go about the hotel, inquiring. The house is so full, and the data I have to go upon are so small, that for some time I have great difficulty in making it understood to whom I am alluding. At length one waiter seems to comprehend.

" A tall and dark gentleman, with a pronounced and very peculiar nose ? Yes; there has been such a one, certainly, in the hotel, but he left at ' grand matin ' this morning; he remained only one night."

" And his name ?"

The garçon shakes his head. "That is unknown, monsieur; he did not inscribe it in the visitor's book."

" What countryman was he ?"

Another shake of the head. "He spoke German, but it was with a foreign accent."

"Whither did he go?"

That also is unknown. Nor can I arrive at any more facts about him.

CHAPTER IV.

A FORTNIGHT has passed; we have been hither and thither; now we are at Lucerne. Peopled with better inhabitants, Lucerne might well do for Heaven. It is drawing towards eventide, and Elizabeth and I are sitting hand in hand on a quiet bench, under the shady linden trees, on a high hill up above the lake. There is nobody to see us, so we sit peaceably hand in hand. Up by the still and solemn monastery we came, with its small and narrow windows, calculated to hinder the holy fathers from promenading curious eyes on the world, the flesh, and the

devil, tripping past them in blue gauze veils :
below us grass and green trees, houses with
high-pitched roofs, little dormer-windows, and
shutters yet greener than the grass ; below us
the lake in its rippleless peace, calm, quiet,
motionless as Bethesda's pool before the coming
of the troubling angel.

"I said it was too good to last," say I, dog-
gedly, "did not I, only yesterday ? Perfect
peace, perfect sympathy, perfect freedom from
nagging worries—when did such a state of
things last more than two days ?"

Elizabeth's eyes are idly fixed on a little
steamer, with a stripe of red along its side,
and a tiny puff of smoke from its funnel,
gliding along and cutting a narrow white
track on Lucerne's sleepy surface.

"This is the fifth false alarm of the gout
having gone to his stomach within the last
two years," continue I, resentfully. "I de-
clare to Heaven, that if it has not really

gone there this time, I'll cut the whole concern."

Let no one cast up their eyes in horror,
imagining that it is my father to whom I am
thus alluding; it is only a great uncle by
marriage, in consideration of whose wealth
and vague promises I have dawdled profession-
less through twenty-eight years of my life.

"You *must* not go," says Elizabeth, giving
my hand an imploring squeeze. "The man in
the Bible said, 'I have married a wife, and
therefore I cannot come;' why should it be a
less valid excuse now a days?"

"If I recollect rightly, it was considered
rather a poor one even then," reply I, dryly.

Elizabeth is unable to contradict this, she
therefore only lifts two pouted lips (Monsieur
Taine objects to the redness of English
women's mouths, but I do not) to be kissed,
and says, "Stay." I am good enough to
comply with her unspoken request, though

I remain firm with regard to her spoken one.

" My dearest child," I say, with an air of worldly experience and superior wisdom, " kisses are very good things—in fact there are few better—but one cannot live upon them."

" Let us try," she says, coaxingly.

" I wonder which would get tired first ?" I say, laughing.   But she only goes on pleading, " Stay, stay."

" How *can* I stay ?" I cry, impatiently; "you talk as if I *wanted* to go ! Do you think it is any pleasanter to me to leave you than to you to be left ? But you know his disposition, his rancorous resentment of fancied neglects.   For the sake of two days' indulgence, must I throw away what will keep us in ease and plenty to the end of our days ?"

" I do not care for plenty," she says, with a

little petulant gesture. "I do not see that
rich people are any happier than poor ones.
Look at the St. Clairs; they have £40,000
a-year, and she is a miserable woman, perfectly miserable, because her face gets red
after dinner."

"There will be no fear of *our* faces getting
red after dinner," say I, grimly, "for we shall
have no dinner for them to get red after."

A pause. My eyes stray away to the
mountains. Pilatus on the right, with his
jagged peak and slender snow-chains about
his harsh neck; hill after hill rising silent,
eternal, like guardian spirits standing hand in
hand around their child, the lake. As I look,
suddenly they have all flushed, as at some
noblest thought, and over all their sullen
faces streams an ineffable rosy joy—a solemn
and wonderful effulgence, such as Israel saw
reflected from the features of the Eternal in
their prophet's transfigured eyes. The un-

utterable peace and stainless beauty of earth
and sky seem to lie softly on my soul.
"Would God I could stay! Would God all
life could be like this!" I say, devoutly, and
the aspiration has the reverent earnestness of
a prayer.

"Why do you say, '*Would God!*'" she
cries, passionately, "when it lies with yourself? Oh my dear love," gently sliding her
hand through my arm, and lifting wetly-
beseeching eyes to my face, "I do not know
why I insist upon it so much—I cannot tell
you myself—I dare say I seem selfish and
unreasonable—but I feel as if your going now
would be the end of all' things—as if——."
She breaks off suddenly.

"My child," say I, thoroughly distressed,
but still determined to have my own way,
"you talk as if I were going for ever and a
day; in a week, at the outside, I shall be back,
and then you will thank me for the very thing

for which you now think me so hard and dis-
obliging."

"Shall I?" she answers, mournfully. "Well,
I hope so."

"You will not be alone, either; you will
have Morris."

"Yes."

"And every day you will write me a long
letter, telling me every single thing that you
do, say, and think."

"Yes."

She answers me gently and obediently; but
I can see that she is still utterly unreconciled
to the idea of my absence.

"What is it that you are afraid of?" I ask,
becoming rather irritated. "What do you
suppose will happen to you?"

She does not answer; only a large tear falls
on my hand, which she hastily wipes away
with her pocket handkerchief, as if afraid of
exciting my wrath.

"Can you give me any good reason why I *should* stay ?" I ask, dictatorially.

"None—none—only—stay—stay !"

But I am resolved *not* to stay. Early the next morning I set off.

CHAPTER V.

THIS time it is not a false alarm; this time it really has gone to his stomach, and, declining to be dislodged thence, kills him. My return is therefore retarded until after the funeral and the reading of the will. The latter is so satisfactory, and my time is so fully occupied with a multiplicity of attendant business, that I have no leisure to regret the delay. I write to Elizabeth, but receive no letters from her. This surprises and makes me rather angry, but does not alarm me. "If she had been ill, if anything had happened, Morris would have written. She never was great at writing, poor little soul. What dear little babyish notes she used to send me during our engagement; perhaps she wishes to punish me for my disobedience to her wishes. Well, *now* she will see who was in the right." I am drawing near her now; I am walking up from the railway station at Lucerne. I am very joyful as I march along under an umbrella, in the grand broad shining of the summer afternoon. I think with pensive passion of the last glimpse I had of my beloved—her small and wistful face looking out from among the thick fair fleece of her long hair—winking away her tears and blowing kisses to me. It is a new sensation to me to have anyone looking tearfully wistful over my departure. I draw near the great glaring Schweizerhof, with its colonnaded, tourist-crowded porch; here are all the pomegranates as I left them, in their green tubs, with their scarlet blossoms, and the dusty oleanders in a row. I look up at our windows;

nobody is looking out from them; they are open, and the curtains are alternately swelled out and drawn in by the softly-playful wind. I run quickly upstairs and burst noisily into the sitting-room. Empty, perfectly empty! I open the adjoining door into the bedroom, crying "Elizabeth! Elizabeth!" but I receive no answer. Empty too. A feeling of indignation creeps over me as I think, " Knowing the time of my return, she might have managed to be indoors." I have returned to the silent sitting-room, where the only noise is the wind still playing hide-and-seek with the curtains. As I look vacantly round my eye catches sight of a letter lying on the table. I pick it up mechanically and look at the address. Good heavens! what can this mean? It is my own, that I sent her two days ago, unopened, with the seal unbroken. Does she carry her resentment so far as not even to open my letters? I spring at the bell and violently ring it. It is

answered by the waiter who has always specially attended us.

" Is madame gone out ?"

The man opens his mouth and stares at
me.

" Madame! Is monsieur then not aware that
madame is no longer at the hotel ?"

" *What ?*"

" On the same day as monsieur, madame
departed."

" *Departed !* Good God! what are you talking about ?" ·

" A few hours after monsieur's departure—I
will not be positive as to the exact time, but
it must have been between one and two
o'clock as the midday *table d'hôte* was in progress—a gentleman came and asked for madame——"

" Yes—be quick."

" I demanded whether I should take up his
card, but he said ' No,' that was unnecessary,

as he was perfectly well known to madame; and, in fact, a short time afterwards, without saying anything to anyone, she departed with him."

" And did not return in the evening ?"

" No, monsieur; madame has not returned since that day."

I clench my hands in an agony of rage and grief. " So this is it! With that pure child-face, with that divine ignorance—only three weeks married—this is the trick she has played me!" I am recalled to myself by a compassionate suggestion from the garçon.

" Perhaps it was the brother of madame."

Elizabeth has no brother, but the remark brings back to me the necessity of self-command. " Very probably," I answer, speaking with infinite difficulty. " What sort of looking gentleman was he ?'

" He was a very tall and dark gentleman with a most peculiar nose—not quite like any nose that I ever saw before—and most singular eyes. Never have I seen a gentleman who at all resembled him."

I sink into a chair, while a cold shudder creeps over me as I think of my poor child's dream—of her fainting fit at Wiesbaden—of her unconquerable dread of and aversion from my departure. And this happened twelve days ago! I catch up my hat, and prepare to rush like a madman in pursuit.

"How did they go?" I ask incoherently; "by train?—driving?—walking?"

"They went in a carriage."

"What direction did they take? Whither did they go?"

He shakes his head. "It is not known."

"It *must* be known," I cry, driven to frenzy by every second's delay. "Of course the driver could tell; where is he?—where can I find him?"

"He did not belong to Lucerne, neither did

the carriage; the gentleman brought them with him."

"But madame's maid," say I, a gleam of hope flashing across my mind; "did she go with her?"

"No, monsieur, she is still here; she was as much surprised as monsieur at madame's departure."

"Send her at once," I cry eagerly; but when she comes I find that she can throw no light on the matter. She weeps noisily and says many irrelevant things, but I can obtain no information from her beyond the fact that she was unaware of her mistress's departure until long after it had taken place, when, surprised at not being rung for at the usual time, she had gone to her room and found it empty, and on inquiring in the hotel, had heard of her sudden departure; that, expecting her to return at night, she had sat up waiting for her till two o'clock in the morning, but that, as I

knew, she had not returned, neither had anything since been heard of her.

Not all my inquiries, not all my cross-
questionings of the whole staff of the hotel,
of the visitors, of the railway officials, of
nearly all the inhabitants of Lucerne and
its environs, procure me a jot more knowledge. On the next few weeks I look back
as on a hellish and insane dream. I can
neither eat nor sleep; I am unable to remain
one moment quiet; my whole existence, my
nights and my days, are spent in seeking,
seeking. Everything that human despair and
frenzied love can do is done by me. I adver-
tise, I communicate with the police, I employ
detectives; but that fatal twelve days' start
for ever baffles me. Only on one occasion do I
obtain one tittle of information. In a village a
few miles from Lucerne the peasants, on the
day in question, saw a carriage driving rapidly
through their little street. It was closed, but

6

through the windows they could see the occupants—a dark gentleman, with the peculiar physiognomy which has been so often described, and on the opposite seat a lady lying apparently in a state of utter insensibility. But even this leads to nothing.

Oh, reader, these things happened twenty years ago; since then I have searched sea and land, but never have I seen my little Elizabeth again.

BEHOLD, IT WAS A DREAM!

BEHOLD, IT WAS A DREAM!

CHAPTER I.

YESTERDAY morning I received the following letter :

"Weston House, Caulfield, ——shire.

"MY DEAR DINAH,—You *must* come : I scorn all your excuses, and see through their flimsiness. I have no doubt that you are much better amused in Dublin, frolicking round ball-rooms with a succession of horse-soldiers, and watching her Majesty's household troops play Polo in the Phœnix Park, but no matter—you *must* come. We have no particular inducements to hold out. We lead an exclusively bucolic, cow-milking, pig-fattening, roast-mutton-eating and to-bed-at-ten-o'clock-going life; but no matter—you *must* come. I want you to see how happy two dull elderly people may be, with no special brightness in their lot to make them so. My old man—he is surprisingly ugly at the first glance, but grows upon one afterwards—sends you his respects, and bids me say that he will meet you at *any* station on *any* day at *any* hour of the day or night. If you succeed in evading our persistence this time, you will be a cleverer woman than I take you for.

" Ever yours affectionately,

"JANE WATSON.

" *August* 15*th.*

" P.S.—We will invite our little scarlet-headed curate to dinner to meet you, so as to soften your fall from the society of the Plungers."

This is my answer :

"MY DEAR JANE,—Kill the fat calf in all haste, and put the bake meats into the oven, for I will come. Do not, however, imagine that I am moved thereunto by the prospect of the bright-headed curate. Believe me, my dear, I am as yet at a distance of ten long good years from an addiction to the minor clergy. If I survive the crossing of that seething, heaving, tumbling abomination, St. George's Channel, you may expect me on Tuesday next. I have been groping for hours in 'Bradshaw's' darkness that may be felt, and I have arrived at length at this twilight result, that I may arrive at your station at 6·55 P.M. But the ways of 'Bradshaw' are not our ways, and I *may* either rush violently past or never attain it. If I do, and if on my arrival I see some rustic vehicle, guided by a astrtlingly ugly gentleman, awaiting me, I

shall know from your wifely description
that it is your 'old man.' Till Tuesday,
then,

"Affectionately yours,

"DINAH BELLAIRS.

"August 17th."

I am as good as my word; on Tuesday I set
off. For four mortal hours and a half I am
disastrously, hideously, diabolically sick. For
four hours and a half I curse the day on which
I was born, the day on which Jane Watson
was born, the day on which her old man was
born, and lastly—but oh! not, *not* leastly—the
day and the deck on which and in which the
Leinster's plunging, courtseying, throbbing
body was born. On arriving at Holyhead,
feeling convinced from my sensations that, as
the French say, I touch my last hour, I indis-
tinctly request to be allowed to stay on board
and *die*, then and there; but as the stewardess
and my maid take a different view of my

situation, and insist upon forcing my cloak and
bonnet on my dying body and limp head, I at
length succeed in staggering on deck and off
the accursed boat. I am then well shaken up
for two or three hours in the Irish mail, and
after crawling along a slow by-line for two or
three hours more, am at length, at 6·55, landed,
battered, tired, dust-blacked, and qualmish, at
the little roadside station of Caulfield. My
maid and I are the only passengers who
descend. The train snorts its slow way on-
wards, and I am left gazing at the calm
crimson death of the August sun, and smelling
the sweet-peas in the station-master's garden
border. I look round in search of Jane's
promised tax-cart, and steel my nerves for the
contemplation of her old man's unlovely
features. But the only vehicle which I
see is a tiny two-wheeled pony carriage, drawn
by a small and tub-shaped bay pony and
driven by a lady in a hat, whose face is turned

expectantly towards me. I go up and recognise my friend, whom I have not seen for two years—not since before she fell in with her old man and espoused him.

"I thought it safest, after all, to come myself," she says with a bright laugh. "My old man looked so handsome this morning, that I thought you would never recognise him from my description. Get in, dear, and let us trot home as quickly as we can.

I comply, and for the next half hour sit (while the cool evening wind is blowing the dust off my hot and jaded face) stealing amazed glances at my companion's cheery features. *Cheery!* That is the very last word that, excepting in an ironical sense, any one would have applied to my friend Jane two years ago. Two years ago Jane was thirty-five, the elderly eldest daughter of a large family, hustled into obscurity, jostled, shelved, by half a dozen younger, fresher sisters; an elderly girl addicted to lachrymose verse about the gone and the dead and the for-ever-lost. Apparently the gone has come back, the dead resuscitated, the for-ever-lost been found again. The peaky sour virgin is transformed into a gracious matron, with a kindly, comely face, pleasure making and pleasure feeling. Oh, Happiness, what powder, or paste, or milk of roses, can make old cheeks young again in the cunning way that you do ? If you would but bide steadily with us we might live for ever, always young and always handsome.

My musings on Jane's metamorphosis, combined with a tired headache, make me somewhat silent, and indeed there is mostly a slackness of conversation between the two dearest allies on first meeting after absence —a sort of hesitating shiver before plunging into the sea of talk that both know lie in readiness for them.

" Have you got your harvest in yet ?" I ask,

more for the sake of not utterly holding my
tongue than from any profound interest in the
subject, as we jog briskly along between the
yellow cornfields, where the dry bound sheaves
are standing in golden rows in the red sunset
light.

"Not yet," answers Jane; "we have only
just begun to cut some of it. However, thank
God, the weather looks as settled as possible;
there is not a streak of watery lilac in the
west."

My headache is almost gone and I am beginning to think kindly of dinner—a subject from
which all day until now my mind has hastily
turned with a sensation of hideous inward
revolt—by the time that the fat pony pulls up
before the old-world dark porch of a modest
little house, which has bashfully hidden its
original face under a veil of crowded clematis
flowers and stalwart ivy. Set as in a picture-
frame by the large drooped ivy-leaves, I see a

tall and moderately hard-featured gentleman
of middle age, perhaps, of the two, rather in-
clining towards elderly, smiling at us a little
shyly.

" This is my old man," cries Jane, stepping
gaily out, and giving him a friendly introduc-
tory pat on the shoulder. "Old man, this is
Dinah."

Having thus been made known to each
other we shake hands, but neither of us can
arrive at anything pretty to say. Then I follow Jane into her little house, the little house
for which she has so happily exchanged her
tenth part of the large and noisy paternal
mansion. It is an old house, and everything
about it has the moderate shabbiness of old
age and long and careful wear. Little thick-
walled rooms, dark and cool, with flowers and
flower scents lying in wait for you everywhere
—a silent, fragrant, childless house. To me,
who have had oily locomotives snorting and

racing through my head all day, its dumb sweetness seems like heaven.

"And now that we have secured you, we do not mean to let you go in a hurry," says Jane hospitably that night at bedtime, lighting the candles on my dressing-table.

"You are determined to make my mouth water, I see," say I, interrupting a yawn to laugh. "Lone lorn me, who have neither old man nor dear little house, nor any prospect of ultimately attaining either."

"But if you honestly are not bored you will stay with us a good bit?" she says, laying her hand with kind entreaty on my sleeve. "St. George's Channel is not lightly to be faced again."

"Perhaps I shall stay until you are obliged to go away yourselves to get rid of me," return I, smiling. "Such things have happened. Yes, without joking, I will stay a month. Then, by the end of a month, if you have not found me out thoroughly, I think I may pass among men for a more amiable woman than I have ever yet had the reputation of."

A quarter of an hour later I am laying down my head among soft and snow-white pillows, and saying to myself that this delicious sensation of utter drowsy repose, of soft darkness and odorous quiet, is cheaply purchased even by the ridiculous anguish which my own sufferings, and—hardly less than my own sufferings—the demoniac sights and sounds afforded by my fellow passengers, caused me on board the accursed *Leinster*—

"Built in the eclipse, and rigged with curses dark."

CHAPTER II.

"WELL, I cannot say that you look much rested," says Jane next morning, coming in to greet me, smiling and fresh—(yes, sceptic of eighteen, even a woman of thirty-seven may look fresh in a print gown on an August morning, when she has a well of lasting quiet happiness inside her)—coming in with a bunch of creamy *gloire de Dijons* in her hand for the breakfast table. "You look infinitely more fagged than you did when I left you last night!"

"Do I?" say I, rather faintly.

"I am afraid you did not sleep much?"

suggests Jane, a little crestfallen at the insult to her feather beds implied by my wakefulness. 'Some people never can sleep the first night in a strange bed, and I stupidly forgot to ask whether you liked the feather bed or mattress at the top."

" Yes, I did sleep," I answer gloomily. " I wish to heaven I had not !"

" Wish—to—heaven—you—had—not ?" repeats Jane slowly, with a slight astonished pause between each word. " My dear child, for what other purpose did you go to bed ?"

" I—I—had bad dreams," say I, shuddering a little and then taking her hand, roses and all, in mine. " Dear Jane, do not think me quite run mad, but—but—have you got a ' Bradshaw ' in the house ?'

" A ' Bradshaw ?' What on earth do you want with ' Bradshaw ?'" says my hostess, her face lengthening considerably and a slight

7

tincture of natural coldness coming into her tone.

"I know it seems rude—insultingly rude," say I, still holding her hand and speaking almost lachrymosely: "but do you know, my dear, I really am afraid that—that—I shall have to leave you—to-day?"

"To leave us?" repeats she, withdrawing her hand and growing angrily red. "What! when not twenty-four hours ago you settled to stay *a month* with us? What have we done between then and now to disgust you with us?"

"Nothing—nothing," cry I, eagerly; "how can you suggest such a thing? I never had a kinder welcome nor ever saw a place that charmed me more; but—but——"

"But what?" asks Jane, her colour subsiding and looking a little mollified.

"It is best to tell the truth, I suppose," say I, sighing, "even though I know that you will laugh at me—will call me vapourish—sottishly superstitious; but I had an awful and hideous dream last night."

"Is that all?" she says, looking relieved, and beginning to arrange her roses in an old china bowl. "And do you think that all dreams are confined to this house? I never heard before of their affecting any one special place more than another. Perhaps no sooner are you back in Dublin, in your own room and your own bed, than you will have a still worse and uglier one."

I shake my head. "But it was about this house—about *you*."

"About *me?*" she says, with an accent of a little aroused interest.

"About you and your husband," I answer earnestly. "Shall I tell it you? Whether you say 'Yes' or 'No' I must. Perhaps it came as a warning; such things have happened. Yes, say what you will, I cannot believe that any vision so consistent—so tangibly real and utterly free from the jumbled incongruities and unlikelinesses of ordinary dreams—could have meant nothing. Shall I begin ?"

" By all means," answers Mrs. Watson, sitting down in an arm-chair and smiling easily. I am quite prepared to listen—and *dis*believe."

" You know," say I, narratively, coming and standing close before her, " how utterly tired out I was when you left me last night. I could hardly answer your questions for yawning. I do not think that I was ten minutes in getting into bed, and it seemed like heaven when I laid my head down on the pillow. I felt as if I should sleep till the Day of Judgment. Well, you know, when one is asleep one has of course no measure of time, and I have no idea what hour it was *really;* but at some time, in the blackest and darkest of the night, I seemed to wake. It appeared as if a noise had woke me—a noise which at first neither frightened nor surprised me in the least, but which seemed quite natural, and which I accounted for in the muddled drowsy way in which one does account for things when half asleep. But as I gradually grew to fuller consciousness I found out, with a cold shudder, that the noise I heard was not one that belonged to the night; nothing that one could lay on wind in the chimney, or mice behind the wainscot, or ill-fitting boards. It was a sound of muffled struggling, and once I heard a sort of choked strangled cry. I sat up in bed, perfectly numbed with fright, and for a moment could hear nothing for the singing of the blood in my head, and the loud battering of my heart against my side. Then I thought that if it were anything bad—if I were going to be murdered—I had at least rather be in the light than the dark, and see in what sort of shape my fate was coming, so I slid

out of bed and threw my dressing-gown over
my shoulders. I had stupidly forgotten, in my
weariness, over night, to put the matches by
the bedside, and could not for the life of me
recollect where they were. Also, my knowledge of the geography of the room was so
small that in the utter blackness, without even
the palest, grayest ray from the window to
help me, I was by no means sure in which
direction the door lay. I can feel *now* the
pain of the blow I gave this right side against
the sharp corner of the table in passing; I was
quite surprised this morning not to find the
mark of a bruise there. At last, in my groping,
I came upon the handle and turned the key in
the lock. It gave a little squeak, and again I
stopped for a moment, overcome by ungovern-
able fear. Then I silently opened the door
and looked out. You know that your door is
exactly opposite mine. By the line of red
light underneath it, I could see that at all

events some one was awake and astir within, for the light was brighter than that given by a night-light. By the broader band of red light on the right side of it I could also perceive that the door was ajar. I stood stock still and listened. The two sounds of struggling and chokedly crying had both ceased. All the noise that remained was that as of some person quietly moving about on unbooted feet. 'Perhaps Jane's dog Smut is ill and she is sitting up with it; she was saying last night, I remember, that she was afraid it was beginning with the distemper. Perhaps either she or her old man have been taken with some trifling temporary sickness. Perhaps the noise of crying out that I certainly heard was one of them fighting with a nightmare.' Trying, by such like suggestions, to hearten myself up, I stole across the passage and peeped in ——"

I pause in my narrative.

"Well?" says Jane, a little impatiently.

᾿ She has dropped her flowers. They lie in odorous dewy confusion in her lap. She is listening rather eagerly. I cover my face with my hands. "Oh! my dear," I cry, "I do not think I can go on. It was *too* dreadful! Now that I am telling it I seem to be doing and hearing it over again ——"

"I do not call it very kind to keep me on the rack," she says, with a rather forced laugh. "Probably I am imagining something much worse than the reality. For heaven's sake speak up! What *did* you see?"

I take hold of her hand and continue. "You know that in your room the bed exactly faces the door. Well, when I looked in, looked in with eyes blinking at first, and dazzled by the long darkness they had been in, it seemed to me as if that bed were only one horrible sheet of crimson; but as my sight grew clearer I saw what it was that caused that frightful impression of universal red——" Again

I pause with a gasp and feeling of oppressed breathing.

"Go on! go on!" cries my companion, leaning forward, and speaking with some petulance. "Are you never going to get to the point?"

"Jane," say I solemnly, "do not laugh at me, nor pooh pooh me, for it is God's truth—as clearly and vividly as I see you now, strong, flourishing, and alive, so clearly, so vividly, with no more of dream haziness nor of contradiction in details than there is in the view I now have of this room and of you—I saw you *both*—you and your husband, lying *dead—murdered*—drowned in your own blood!"

"What, both of us?" she says, trying to laugh, but her healthy cheek has rather paled.

"Both of you," I answer, with growing excitement. "You, Jane, had evidently been the one first attacked—taken off in your sleep —for you were lying just as you would have lain in slumber, only that across your throat from there to there " (touching first one ear and then the other), " there was a huge and yawning gash."

" Pleasant," replies she, with a slight shiver.

"I never saw any one dead," continue I earnestly, " never until last night. I had not the faintest idea how dead people looked, even people who died quietly, nor has any picture ever given me at all a clear conception of death's dread look. How then could I have *imagined* the hideous contraction and distortion of feature, the staring starting open eyes —glazed yet agonized— the tightly clenched teeth that go to make up the picture, that is *now, this very minute,* standing out in ugly vividness before my mind's eye ?" I stop, but she does not avail herself of the pause to make any remark, neither does she look any longer at all laughingly inclined.

" And yet," continue I, with a voice shaken

by emotion, " it was *you, very* you, not partly
you and partly some one else, as is mostly the
case in dreams, but as much *you,* as the *you* I
am touching now " (laying my finger on her
arm as I speak).

"And my old man, Robin," says poor Jane,
rather tearfully, after a moment's silence,
" what about him ? Did you see him ? Was
he dead too ?"

" It was evidently he whom I had heard
struggling and crying," I answer with a strong
shudder, which I cannot keep down, " for it
was clear that he had fought for his life. He
was lying half on the bed and half on the
floor, and one clenched hand was grasping a
great piece of the sheet; he was lying head
downwards, as if, after his last struggle, he
had fallen forwards. All his grey hair was
reddened and stained, and I could see that the
rift in his throat was as deep as that in yours."

" I wish you would stop," cries Jane, pale as

ashes, and speaking with an accent of unwill-
ing terror; "you are making me quite sick!"

"I *must* finish," I answer earnestly, "since
it has come in time I am sure it has come for
some purpose. Listen to me till the end; it
is very near." She does not speak, and I take
her silence for assent. "I was staring at you
both in a stony way," I go on, "feeling—if I
felt at all—that I was turning idiotic with
horror—standing in exactly the same spot,
with my neck craned to look round the door,
and my eyes unable to stir from that hideous
scarlet bed, when a slight noise, as of some one
cautiously stepping on the carpet, turned my
stony terror into a living quivering agony. I
looked and saw a man with his back towards
me walking across the room from the bed to
the dressing-table. He was dressed in the
dirty fustian of an ordinary workman, and in
his hand he held a red wet sickle. When he
reached the dressing-table he laid it down on

the floor beside him, and began to collect all the rings, open the cases of the bracelets, and hurry the trinkets of all sorts into his pockets. While he was thus busy I caught a full view of the reflection of the face in the glass——" I stop for breath, my heart is panting almost as hardly as it seemed to pant during the awful moments I am describing.

"What was he like—what was he like?" cries Jane, greatly excited. "Did you see him distinctly enough to recollect his features again? Would you know him again if you saw him?"

"Should I know my own face if I saw it in the glass?" I ask scornfully. "I see every line of it *now* more clearly than I do yours, though that is before my eyes, and the other only before my memory——"

"Well, what was he like?—be quick, for heaven's sake."

"The first moment that I caught sight of

him," continue I, speaking quickly, "I felt certain that he was Irish; to no other nationality could such a type of face have belonged. His wild rough hair fell down over his forehead, reaching his shagged and overhanging brows. He had the wide grinning slit of a mouth—the long nose, the cunningly twinkling eyes—that one so often sees, in combination with a shambling gait and ragged tail-coat, at the railway stations or in the harvest fields at this time of year." A pause. "I do not know how it came to me," I go on presently; "but I felt as convinced as if I had been told—as if I had known it for a positive fact—that he was one of your own labourers—one of your own harvest men. Have you any Irishmen working for you ?"

"Of course we have," answers Jane, rather sharply, "but that proves nothing. Do not they, as you observed just now, come over in droves at this time of the year for the harvest?"

" I am sorry," say I, sighing. " I wish you had not. Well, let me finish; I have just done—I had been holding the door-handle mechanically in my hand; I suppose I pulled it unconsciously towards me, for the door hinge creaked a little, but quite audibly. To my unspeakable horror the man turned round and saw me. Good God! he would cut my throat too with that red, *red* reaping hook! I tried to get into the passage and lock the door, but the key was on the inside. I tried to scream, I tried to run; but voice and legs disobeyed me. The bed and room and man began to dance before me; a black earthquake seemed to swallow me up, and I suppose I fell down in a swoon. When I awoke *really* the blessed morning had come, and a robin was singing outside my window on an apple bough. There—you have it all, and now let me look for a ' Bradshaw,' for I am so frightened and unhinged that go I must."

CHAPTER III.

" I MUST own that it has taken away appe-
tite," I say, with rather a sickly smile, as we
sit round the breakfast table. " I assure you
that I mean no insult to your fresh eggs and
bread-and-butter, but I simply *cannot* eat."

" It certainly was an exceptionally dreadful
dream," says Jane, whose colour has returned,
and who is a good deal fortified and reassured
by the influences of breakfast and of her
husband's scepticism; for a condensed and
shortened version of my dream has been told
to him, and he has easily laughed it to scorn.
" Exceptionally dreadful, chiefly from its ex-

treme consistency and precision of detail. But
still, you know, dear, one has had hideous
dreams oneself times out of mind and they
never came to anything. I remember once I
dreamt that all my teeth came out in my
mouth at once—double ones and all; but that
was ten years ago, and they still keep their
situations, nor did I about that time lose any
friend, which they say such a dream is a sign
of."

" You say that some unaccountable instinct
told you that the hero of your dream was one
of my own men," says Robin, turning towards
me with a covert smile of benevolent contempt
for my superstitiousness; "did not I understand you to say so ?"

" Yes," reply I, not in the least shaken by his
hardly-veiled disbelief. " I do not know how
it came to me, but I was as much persuaded of
that, and am so still, as I am of my own
identity."

"I will tell you of a plan then to prove the truth of your vision," returns he, smiling. "I will take you through the fields this morning and you shall see all my men at work, both the ordinary staff and the harvest casuals, Irish and all. If amongst them you find the counterpart of Jane's and my murderer" (a smile) "I will promise *then*—no, not even *then* can I promise to believe you, for there is such a family likeness between all Irishmen, at all events, between all the Irishmen that one sees *out* of Ireland."

"Take me," I say, eagerly, jumping up; "now, this *minute!* You cannot be more anxious nor half so anxious to prove me a false prophet as I am to be proved one."

"I am quite at your service," he answers, "as soon as you please. Jenny, get your hat and come too."

"And if we do *not* find him," says Jane, smiling playfully—"I think I am growing pretty easy on that head—you will promise to eat a great deal of luncheon and never *mention* 'Bradshaw' again ?"

" I promise," reply I, gravely. " And if, on the other hand, we *do* find him, you will promise to put no more obstacles in the way of my going, but will let me depart in peace without taking any offence thereat ?"

" It is a bargain," she says gaily. " Witness, Robin."

So we set off in the bright dewiness of the morning on our walk over Robin's farm. It is a grand harvest day, and the whitened sheaves are everywhere drying, drying in the genial sun. We have been walking for an hour and both Jane and I are rather tired. The sun beats with all his late-summer strength on our heads and takes the force and spring out of our hot limbs.

" The hour of triumph is approaching," says Robin, with a quiet smile, as we draw near an

8—2

open gate through which a loaded wain, shedding ripe wheat ears from its abundance as it crawls along, is passing. "And time for it too; it is a quarter past twelve and you have been on your legs for fully an hour. Miss Bellairs, you must make haste and find the murderer, for there is only one more field to do it in."

"Is not there?" I cry eagerly, "Oh, I *am* glad! Thank God, I begin to breathe again."

We pass through the open gate and begin to tread across the stubble, for almost the last load has gone.

"We must get nearer the hedge," says Robin, "or you will not see their faces; they are all at dinner."

We do as he suggests. In the shadow of the hedge we walk close in front of the row of heated labourers, who, sitting or lying on the hedge bank, are eating unattractive looking dinners. I scan one face after another —bonest bovine English faces. I have seen a hundred thousand faces *like* each one of the faces now before me—very like, but the exact counterpart of none. We are getting to the end of the row, I beginning to feel rather ashamed, though infinitely relieved, and to smile at my own expense. I look again, and my heart suddenly stands still and turns to stone within me. He is *there!*—not a hand-breadth from me! Great God! how well I have remembered his face, even to the unsightly smallpox seams, the shagged locks, the grinning slit mouth, the little sly base eyes. He is employed in no murderous occupation *now;* he is harmlessly cutting hunks of coarse bread and fat cold bacon with a clasp knife, but yet I have no more doubt that it is *he*—he whom I saw with the crimsoned sickle in his stained hand—than I have that it is I who am stonily, shiveringly, staring at him."

" Well, Miss Bellairs, who was right ?" asks Robin's cheery voice at my elbow. " Perish

'Bradshaw' and all his labyrinths! Are you satisfied now? Good heavens!" (catching a sudden sight of my face) "How white you are! Do you mean to say that you have found him at last? Impossible!"

" Yes, I have found him," I answer in a low and unsteady tone. " I knew I should. Look, there he is!—close to us, the third from the end."

I turn away my head, unable to bear the hideous recollections and associations that the sight of the man calls up, and I suppose that they both look.

" Are you sure that you are not letting your imagination carry you away?" asks he presently, in a tone of gentle kindly remonstrance. " As I said before these fellows are all so much alike; they have all the same look of debased squalid cunning. Oblige me by looking once again, so as to be quite sure."

I obey. Reluctantly I look at him once again. Apparently, becoming aware that he is the object of our notice, he lifts his small dull eyes and looks back at me. It is the same face—they are the same eyes that turned from the plundered dressing-table to catch sight of me last night. "There is no mistake," I answer, shuddering from head to foot. "Take me away, please—as quick as you can—out of the field—home!"

They comply, and over the hot fields and through the hot noon air we step silently homewards. As we reach the cool and ivied porch of the house I speak for the first time. "You believe me *now?*"

He hesitates. "I was staggered for a moment, I will own," he answers, with candid gravity; "but I have been thinking it over, and on reflection I have come to the conclusion that the highly excited state of your imagination is answerable for the heightening of the resemblance which exists between all the Irish of that class into an identity with the particular Irishman you dreamed of, and whose face (by your own show-ing) you only saw dimly reflected in the glass."

" *Not* dimly," repeat I emphatically, " unless I now see that sun dimly " (pointing to him, as he gloriously, blindingly blazes from the sky). " You will not be warned by me then ?" I continue passionately, after an interval. " You will run the risk of my dream coming true—you will stay on here in spite of it ? Oh, if I could persuade you to go from home —anywhere—anywhere—for a time, until the danger was past !"

" And leave the harvest to itself ?" answers he, with a smile of quiet sarcasm ; " be a loser of two hundred or three hundred pounds, probably, and a laughing-stock to my ac-quaintance into the bargain, and all for— what ? A dream—a fancy—a nightmare !"

" But do you know anything of the man ?—
of his antecedents ?—of his character ?" I
persist eagerly.

He shrugs his shoulders.

" Nothing whatever; nothing to his dis-
advantage, certainly. He came over with a
lot of others a fortnight ago, and I engaged
him for the harvesting. For anything I
have heard to the contrary, he is a simple in-
offensive fellow enough."

I am silenced, but not convinced. I turn
to Jane. " You remember your promise : you
will now put no more hindrances in the way
of my going ?"

"You do not mean to say that you are
going, really ?" says Jane, who is looking
rather awed by what she calls the surprising
coincidence, but is still a good deal heartened
up by her husband's want of faith.

" I do," reply I, emphatically. " I should
go stark staring mad if I were to sleep

another night in that room. I shall go to Chester to-night, and cross to-morrow from Holyhead."

I do as I say. I make my maid, to her extreme surprise, repack my just unpacked wardrobe and take an afternoon train to Chester. As I drive away with bag and baggage down the leafy lane, I look back and see my two friends standing at their gate. Jane is leaning her head on her old man's shoulder, and looking rather wistfully after me: an expression of mingled regret for my departure and vexation at my folly clouding their kind and happy faces. At least my last living recollection of them is a pleasant one.

CHAPTER IV.

THE joy with which my family welcome my return is largely mingled with surprise, but still more largely with curiosity, as to the cause of my so sudden reappearance. But I keep my own counsel. I have a reluctance to give the real reason, and possess no inventive faculty in the way of lying, so I give none. I say, "I *am* back : is not that enough for you ? Set your minds at rest, for that is as much as you will ever know about the matter."

For one thing, I am occasionally rather ashamed of my conduct. It is not that the impression produced by my dream is *effaced*, but that absence and distance from the scene and the persons of it have produced their natural weakening effect. Once or twice during the voyage, when writhing in laughable torments in the ladies' cabin of the steamboat, I said to myself, "Most likely you are a fool!" I therefore continually ward off the cross-questionings of my family with what defensive armour of silence and evasion I may.

"I feel convinced it was the husband," says one of my sisters, after a long catechism, which, as usual, has resulted in nothing. "You are too loyal to your friend to own it, but I always felt sure that any man who could take compassion on that poor peevish old Jane must be some wonderful freak of nature. Come, confess. Is not he a cross between an ourang-outang and a Methodist parson?"

"He is nothing of the kind," reply I, in some heat, recalling the libelled Robin's clean fresh-coloured *human* face. " You will be very lucky if you ever secure any one half so kind, pleasant, and gentleman-like."

Three days after my return, I receive a letter from Jane :

"Weston House, Caulfield.

" MY DEAR DINAH,—I hope you are safe home again, and that you have made up your mind that two crossings of St. George's Channel within forty-eight hours are almost as bad as having your throat cut, according to the programme you laid out for *us.* I have good news for you. Our murderer elect is *gone.* After hearing of the connection that there was to be between us, Robin naturally was rather interested in him, and found out his name, which is the melodious one of Watty Doolan. After asking his name he asked other things about him, and finding that he never did a stroke of work and was inclined to be tipsy and quarrelsome, he paid and packed him off at once. He is now, I hope, on his way back to his native shores, and if he murder anybody it will be *you*, my dear. Good-bye, Dinah. Hardly yet have I forgiven you for the way in which you frightened me with your graphic description of poor Robin and me, with our heads loose and waggling.

    " Ever yours affectionately,

        " JANE WATSON."

I fold up this note with a feeling of exceeding relief, and a thorough faith that I have been a superstitious hysterical fool. More resolved than ever am I to keep the reason for my return profoundly secret from my family. The next morning but one we are all in the breakfast-room after breakfast, hanging about, and looking at the papers. My sister has just thrown down the *Times*, with a pettish exclamation that there is nothing in it, and that it

really is not worth while paying threepence a
day to see nothing but advertisements and
police reports. I pick it up as she throws it
down, and look listlessly over its tall columns
from top to bottom. Suddenly my listlessness
vanishes. What is this that I am reading ?—
this in staring capitals ?

"SHOCKING TRAGEDY AT CAULFIELD.
DOUBLE MURDER."

I am in the middle of the paragraph before
I realise what it is.

"From an early hour of the morning this
village has been the scene of deep and painful
excitement in consequence of the discovery of
the atrocious murder of Mr. and Mrs. Watson,
of Weston House, two of its most respected
inhabitants. It appears that the deceased had
retired to rest on Tuesday night at their usual
hour, and in their usual health and spirits.
The housemaid, on going to call them at the

accustomed hour on Wednesday morning, received no answer, in spite of repeated knocking. She therefore at length opened the door
and entered. The rest of the servants, at-
tracted by her cries, rushed to the spot, and
found the unfortunate gentleman and lady
lying on the bed with their throats cut from
ear to ear. Life must have been extinct for
some hours, as they were both perfectly cold.
The room presented a hideous spectacle, being
literally swimming in blood. A reaping hook,
evidently the instrument with which the crime
was perpetrated, was picked up near the door.
An Irish labourer of the name of Watty
Doolan, discharged by the lamented gentleman
a few days ago on account of misconduct, has
already been arrested on strong suspicion, as at
an early hour on Wednesday morning he was
seen by a farm labourer, who was going to his
work, washing his waistcoat at a retired spot
in the stream which flows through the meadows
below the scene of the murder. On being
apprehended and searched, several small articles
of jewelry, identified as having belonged to
Mr. Watson, were discovered in his pos-
session."

I drop the paper and sink into a chair, feeling deadly sick.

So you see that my dream came true, after all.

The facts narrated in the above story occurred in Ireland. The only liberty I have taken with them is in transplanting them to England.

POOR PRETTY BOBBY.

9—2

POOR PRETTY BOBBY.

"YES, my dear, you may not believe me, but I can assure you that you cannot dislike old women more, nor think them more contemptible supernumeraries, than I did when I was your age."

This is what old Mrs. Wentworth says—the old lady so incredibly tenacious of life (incredibly as it seems to me at eighteen) as to have buried a husband and five strong sons, and yet still to eat her dinner with hearty relish, and laugh at any such jokes as are spoken loudly enough to reach her dulled ears. This is what she says, shaking the while her head, which—

poor old soul—is already shaking a good deal
involuntarily. I am sitting close beside her
arm-chair, and have been reading aloud to
her; but as I cannot succeed in pitching
my voice so as to make her hear satisfactorily,
by mutual consent the book has been dropped
in my lap, and we have betaken ourselves
to conversation.

"I never said I disliked old women, did
I?" reply I evasively, being too truthful
altogether to deny the soft impeachment.
"What makes you think I do? They are
infinitely preferable to old men; I do distinctly dislike *them*."

"A fat, bald, deaf old woman," continues
she, not heeding me, and speaking with slow
emphasis, while she raises one trembling hand
to mark each unpleasant adjective; "if in the
year '2 any one had told me that I should have
lived to be that, I think I should have killed
them or myself! and yet now I am all three."

"You are not *very* deaf," say I politely
—(the fatness and baldness admit of no civi-
lities consistent with veracity)—but I raise
my voice to pay the compliment.

"In the year '2 I was seventeen," she says,
wandering off into memory. "Yes, my dear,
I am just fifteen years older than the century
and *it* is getting into its dotage, is not it?
The year '2—ah! that was just about the
time that I first saw my poor Bobby! Poor
pretty Bobby."

"And who *was* Bobby?" ask I, pricking up
my ears, and scenting, with the keen nose of
youth, a dead-love idyll; an idyll of which
this poor old hill of unsteady flesh was
the heroine.

"I must have told you the tale a hundred
times, have not I?" she asks, turning her
old dim eyes towards me. "A curious tale,
say what you will, and explain it how you
will. I think I *must* have told you; but

indeed I forgot to whom I tell my old stories
and to whom I do not. Well, my love, you
must promise to stop me if you have heard it
before, but to me, you know, these old things
are so much clearer than the things of
yesterday."

"You never told me, Mrs. Hamilton," I say,
and say truthfully; for being a new acquaintance I really have not been made acquainted
with Bobby's history. "Would you mind
telling it me now, if you are sure that it
would not bore you ?"

"Bobby," she repeats softly to herself,
"Bobby. I daresay you do not think it a
very pretty name ?"

"N—not particularly," reply I honestly.
"To tell you the truth, it rather reminds me
of a policeman."

"I daresay," she answers quietly; "and
yet in the year '2 I grew to think it the
handsomest, dearest name on earth.   Well,

if you like, I will begin at the beginning and
tell you how that came about."

"Do," say I, drawing a stocking out of my
pocket, and thriftily beginning to knit to assist
me in the process of listening.

"In the year '2 we were at war with
France—you know that, of course. It seemed
then as if war were our normal state; I could
hardly remember a time when Europe had
been at peace. In these days of stagnant
quiet it appears as if people's kith and kin
always lived out their full time and died
in their beds. *Then* there was hardly a house
where there was not one dead, either in battle,
or of his wounds after battle, or of some
dysentery or ugly parching fever. As for us,
we had always been a soldier family—always;
there was not one of us that had ever worn
a black gown or sat upon a high stool with
a pen behind his ear. I had lost uncles and
cousins by the half-dozen and dozen, but,

for my part, I did not much mind, as I knew very little about them, and black was more becoming wear to a person with my bright colour than anything else."

At the mention of her bright colour I unintentionally lift my eyes from my knitting, and contemplate the yellow bagginess of the poor old cheek nearest me. Oh, Time! Time! what absurd and dirty turns you play us! What do you do with all our fair and goodly things when you have stolen them from us? In what far and hidden treasure-house do you store them?

"But I did care very much—very exceedingly—for my dear old father—not so old either—younger than my eldest boy was, when he went; he would have been forty-two if he had lived three days longer. Well, well, child, you must not let me wander; you must keep me to it. He was not a soldier, was not my father; he was a sailor, a post-captain in his Majesty's navy and commanded the ship *Thunderer* in the Channel fleet.

"I had struck seventeen in the year '2, as I said before, and had just come home from being finished at a boarding-school of repute in those days, where I had learnt to talk the prettiest *ancien régime* French and to hate Bonaparte with unchristian violence from a little ruined *émigre maréchale;* had also, with infinite expenditure of time, labour, and Berlin wool, wrought out 'Abraham's Sacrifice of Isaac' [and 'Jacob's First Kiss to Rachel,' in finest cross-stitch. Now I had bidden adieu to learning; had inly resolved never to disinter 'Télémaque' and Thompson's 'Seasons' from the bottom of my trunk; had taken a holiday from all my accomplishments with the exception of cross-stitch, to which I still faithfully adhered—and indeed, on the day I am going to mention, I recollect that I was hard at work on Judas Iscariot's face in

Leonardo da Vinci's 'Last Supper'—hard at work at it, sitting in the morning sunshine, on a straight-backed chair. We had flatter backs in those days; our shoulders were not made round by lolling in easy-chairs; indeed, no *then* upholsterer made a chair that it was possible to loll in. My father rented a house near Plymouth at that time, an in-and-out *nooky* kind of old house—no doubt it has fallen to pieces long years ago—a house all set round with unnumbered flowers, and about which the rooks clamoured all together from the windy elm tops. I was labouring in flesh-coloured wool on Judas's left cheek, when the door opened and my mother entered. She looked as if something had freshly pleased her, and her eyes were smiling. In her hand she held an open and evidently just-read letter.

"'A messenger has come from Plymouth,' she says, advancing quickly and joyfully towards me. "Your father will be here this afternoon.'

"'*This afternoon !*' cry I, at the top of my voice, pushing away my heavy work-frame. 'How delightful! But how ?—how can that happen ?'

"'They have had a brush with a French privateer,' she answers, sitting down on another straight-backed chair, and looking again over the large square letter, destitute of envelope, for such things were not in those days, ' and then they succeeded in taking her. Yet they were a good deal knocked about in the process, and have had to put into Plymouth to refit, so he will be here this afternoon for a few hours.'

"'Hurrah !' cry I, rising, holding out my scanty skirts, and beginning to dance.

"'Bobby Gerard is coming with him,' continues my mother, again glancing at her despatch. 'Poor boy, he has had a shot through his right arm, which has broken the bone, so your father is bringing him here for us to nurse him well again.'

" I stop in my dancing.

" 'Hurrah again !' I say brutally. 'I do not mean about his arm; of course I am very sorry for that; but at all events, I shall see him at last. I shall see whether he is like his picture, and whether it is not as egregiously flattered as I have always suspected.'

" There were no photographs you know in those days—not even hazy daguerreotypes— it was fifty good years too soon for them. The picture to which I allude is a miniature, at which I had stolen many a deeply longingly admiring glance in its velvet case. It is almost impossible for a miniature not to flatter. To the most coarse-skinned and mealy-potato-faced people it cannot help giving cheeks of the texture of a rose-leaf and brows of the grain of finest marble.

"'Yes,' replies my mother, absently, 'so you will. Well, I must be going to give orders about his room. He would like one looking on the garden best, do not you think, Phœbe?—one where he could smell the flowers and hear the birds?'

"Mother goes, and I fall into a meditation. Bobby Gerard is an orphan. A few years ago his mother, who was an old friend of my father's—who knows! perhaps an old love—feeling her end drawing nigh, had sent for father, and had asked him, with eager dying tears, to take as much care of her pretty forlorn boy as he could, and to shield him a little in his tender years from the evils of this wicked world, and to be to him a wise and kindly guardian, in the place of those natural ones that God had taken. And father had promised, and when he promised there was small fear of his not keeping his word.

"This was some years ago, and yet I had

never seen him nor he me; he had been almost
always at sea and I at school. I had heard
plenty about him—about his sayings, his wag-
geries, his mischievousness, his soft-hearted-
ness, and his great and unusual comeliness;
but his outward man, save as represented in
that stealthily peeped-at miniature, had I never
seen. They were to arrive in the afternoon;
but long before the hour at which they were
due I was waiting with expectant impatience
to receive them. I had changed my dress, and
had (though rather ashamed of myself) put
on everything of most becoming that my
wardrobe afforded. If you were to see me as
I stood before the glass on that summer afternoon you would not be able to contain your
laughter; the little boys in the street would
run after me throwing stones and hooting; but
then—according to the *then* fashion and stan-
dard of gentility—I was all that was most ele-
gant and *comme il faut.* Lately it has been

the mode to puff oneself out with unnatural and improbable protuberances; *then* one's great life-object was to make oneself appear as scrimping as possible—to make oneself look as flat as if one had been ironed. Many people *damped* their clothes to make them stick more closely to them, and to make them define more distinctly the outline of form and limbs. One's waist was under one's arm's; the sole object of which seemed to be to outrage nature by pushing one's bust up into one's chin, and one's legs were revealed through one's scanty drapery with startling candour as one walked or sat. I remember once standing with my back to a bright fire in our long drawing-room, and seeing myself reflected in a big mirror at the other end. I was so thinly clad that I was transparent, and could see through myself. Well, in the afternoon in question I was dressed quite an hour and a half too soon. I had a narrow little white

gown, which clung successfully tight and
close to my figure, and which was of so moderate a length as to leave visible my ankles
and my neatly-shod and cross-sandled feet.
I had long mittens on my arms, black, and
embroidered on the backs in coloured silks;
and above my hair, which at the back was
scratched up to the top of my crown, towered
a tremendous tortoise-shell comb; while on
each side of my face modestly drooped a
bunch of curls, nearly meeting over my nose.

" My figure was full—ah! my dear, I have
always had a tendency to fat, and you see
what it has come to—and my pink cheeks
were more deeply brightly rosy than usual. I
had looked out at every upper window, so as
to have the furthest possible view of the road.

" I had walked in my thin shoes half way
down the drive, so as to command a turn,
which, from the house, impeded my vision,
when, at last, after many tantalising false

alarms, and just five minutes later than the time mentioned in the letter, the high-swung, yellow - bodied, post - chaise hove in sight, dragged—briskly jingling—along by a pair of galloping horses. Then, suddenly, shyness overcame me—much as I loved my father, it was more as my personification of all knightly and noble qualities than from much personal acquaintance with him—and I fled.

"I remained in my room until I thought I had given them ample time to get through the first greetings and settle down into quiet talk. Then, having for one last time run my fingers through each ringlet of my two curl bunches, I stole diffidently downstairs.

"There was a noise of loud and gay voices issuing from the parlour, but, as I entered, they all stopped talking and turned to look at me.

"'And so this is Phœbe!' cries my father's jovial voice, as he comes towards me, and heartily kisses me. 'Good Lord, how time flies! It does not seem more than three months since I saw the child, and yet then she was a bit of a brat in trousers, and long bare legs!'

"At this allusion to my late mode of attire, I laugh, but I also feel myself growing scarlet.

"'Here, Bobby!' continues my father, taking me by the hand, and leading me towards a sofa on which a young man is sitting beside my mother; 'this is my little lass that you have so often heard of. Not such a very little one, after all, is she? Do not be shy, my boy; you will not see such a pretty girl every day of your life—give her a kiss.'

"My eyes are on the ground, but I am aware that the young man rises, advances (not unwillingly, as it seems to me), and bestows a kiss, somewhere or other on my face. I am not quite clear *where*, as I think the curls impede him a good deal.

" Thus, before ever I saw Bobby, before ever I knew what manner of man he was, I was kissed by him.   That was a good beginning, was not it ?

"After these salutations are over, we subside again into conversation—I sitting beside my father, with his arm round my waist, sitting modestly silent, and peeping every now and then under my eyes, as often as I think I may do so safely unobserved, at the young fellow opposite me. I am instituting an inward comparison between Nature and Art : between the real live man and the miniature that undertakes to represent him.   The first result of this inspection is disappointment, for where are the lovely smooth roses and lilies that I have been wont to connect with Bobby Gerard's name ?   There are no roses in his cheek, certainly ; they are paleish—from his wound, as I conjecture ; but even before that accident, if there were roses at all, they must have been

mahogany-coloured ones, for the salt sea winds
and the high summer sun have tanned his fair
face to a rich reddish, brownish, copperish
hue. But in some things the picture lied not.
There is the brow more broad than high; the
straight fine nose; the brave and joyful blue
eyes, and the mouth with its pretty curling
smile. On the whole, perhaps, I am not dis-
appointed.

"By-and-by father rises, and steps out into
the verandah, where the canary birds hung
out in their cages are noisily praising God
after their manner. Mother follows him. I
should like to do the same; but a sense of
good manners, and a conjecture that possibly
my parents may have some subjects to discuss,
on which they would prefer to be without the
help of my advice, restrain me. I therefore
remain, and so does the invalid.

CHAPTER II.

" For some moments the silence threatens to
remain unbroken between us; for some moments the subdued sound of father's and
mother's talk from among the rosebeds and
the piercing clamour of the canaries—fish-
wives among birds—are the only noises that
salute our ears. Noise we make none ourselves. My eyes are reading the muddled
pattern of the Turkey carpet; I do not know
what his are doing. Small knowledge have I
had of men saving the dancing-master at our
school; a beautiful new youth is almost as
great a novelty to me as to Miranda, and I am

a good deal gawkier than she was under the new experience. I think he must have made a vow that he would not speak first. I feel myself swelling to double my normal size with confusion and heat; at last, in desperation, I look up, and say sententiously, 'You have been wounded, I believe ?'

"'Yes, I have.'

"He might have helped me by answering more at large, might not he ? But now that I am having a good look at him, I see that he is rather red too. Perhaps he also feels gawky and swollen; the idea encourages me.

"'Did it hurt very badly ?'

"'N—not so very much.'

"'I should have thought that you ought to have been in bed,' say I, with a motherly air of solicitude.

"'Should you, why ?'

"'I thought that when people broke their

limbs they had to stay in bed till they were mended again.'

"'But mine was broken a week ago,' he answers, smiling and showing his straight white teeth—ah, the miniature was silent about *them!* 'You would not have had me stay in bed a whole week like an old woman?'

"'I expected to have seen you much *iller,*' say I, beginning to feel more at my ease, and with a sensible diminution of that unpleasant swelling sensation. 'Father said in his note that we were to nurse you well again; that sounded as if you were *quite* ill.'

"'Your father always takes a great deal too much care of me,' he says, with a slight frown and darkening of his whole bright face. 'I might be sugar or salt.'

"'And very kind of him, too,' I cry, firing up. 'What motive beside your own good can he have for looking after you? I call you rather ungrateful.'

"'Do you?' he says calmly, and without apparent resentment. 'But you are mistaken. I am not ungrateful. However, naturally, you do not understand.'

"'Oh, indeed!' reply I, speaking rather shortly, and feeling a little offended, 'I dare say not.'

"Our talk is taking a somewhat hostile tone; to what further amenities we might have proceeded is unknown; for at this point father and mother reappear through the window, and the necessity of conversing with each other at all ceases.

"Father staid till evening, and we all supped together, and I was called upon to sit by Bobby, and cut up his food for him, as he was disabled from doing it for himself. Then, later still, when the sun had set, and all his evening reds and purples had followed him, when the night flowers were scenting all the garden, and the shadows lay about, enormously long in the summer moonlight, father got into the post-chaise again, and drove away through the black shadows and the faint clear shine, and Bobby stood at the hall door watching him, with his arm in a sling and a wistful smile on lips and eyes.

"'Well, we are not left *quite* desolate this time,' says mother, turning with rather tearful laughter to the young man. 'You wish that we were, do not you, Bobby?'

"'You would not believe me, if I answered "No," would you?' he asks, with the same still smile.

"'He is not very polite to us, is he, Phœbe?'

"'You would not wish me to be polite in such a case,' he replies, flushing. 'You would not wish me to be *glad* at missing the chance of seeing any of the fun?'

"But Mr. Gerard's eagerness to be back at his post delays the probability of his being able to return thither. The next day he has a feverish attack, the day after he is worse; the day after that worse still, and in fine, it is between a fortnight and three weeks before he also is able to get into a post-chaise and drive away to Plymouth. And meanwhile mother and I nurse him and cosset him, and make him odd and cool drinks out of herbs and field-flowers, whose uses are now disdained or forgotten. I do not mean any offence to you, my dear, but I think that young girls in those days were less squeamish and more truly delicate than they are now-adays. I remember once I read 'Humphrey Clinker' aloud to my father, and we both highly relished and laughed over its jokes; but I should not have understood one of the darkly unclean allusions in that French book your brother left here one day. *You* would think it very unseemly to enter the bedroom of a strange young man, sick or well; but as for me, I spent whole nights in Bobby's,

watching him and tending him with as little
false shame as if he had been my brother. I
can hear *now*, more plainly than the song
you sang me an hour ago, the slumberous
buzzing of the great brown-coated summer
bees in his still room, as I sat by his bedside
watching his sleeping face, as he dreamt un-
quietly, and clenched, and again unclenched,
his nervous hands. I think he was back in
the *Thunderer.* I can see *now* the little
close curls of his sunshiny hair straggling
over the white pillow. And then there came
a good and blessed day, when he was out of
danger, and then another, a little further on,
when he was up and dressed, and he and I
walked forth into the hayfield beyond the
garden—reversing the order of things—*he*,
leaning on *my* arm; and a good plump solid
arm it was. We walked out under the heavy-
leaved horse-chestnut trees, and the old and
rough-barked elms. The sun was shining all

this time, as it seems to me. I do not believe that in those old days there were the same cold unseasonable rains as now; there were soft showers enough to keep the grass green and the flowers undrooped; but I have no association of overcast skies and untimely deluges with those long and azure days. We sat under a haycock, on the shady side, and indolently watched the hot haymakers—the shirt-sleeved men, and burnt and bare-armed women, tossing and raking; while we breathed the blessed country air, full of adorable scents, and crowded with little happy and pretty-winged insects.

"'In three days,' says Bobby, leaning his elbow in the hay, and speaking with an eager smile, 'three days at the furthest, I may go back again; may not I, Phœbe?'

"'Without doubt,' reply I, stiffly, pulling a dry and faded ox-eye flower out of the odorous mound beside me; 'for my part, I do not see

why you should not go to-morrow, or indeed—
if we could send into Plymouth for a chaise—
this afternoon; you are so thin that you look
all mouth and eyes, and you can hardly stand,
without assistance, but these, of course, are
trifling drawbacks, and I daresay would be
rather an advantage on board ship than other-
wise.'

"'You are angry!' he says, with a sort of
laugh in his deep eyes. 'You look even pret-
tier when you are angry than when you are
pleased.'

"'It is no question of my looks,' I say, still
in some heat, though mollified by the irrelevant compliment.

"'For the second time you are thinking me
ungrateful,' he says, gravely; 'you do not tell
me so in so many words, because it is towards
yourself that my ingratitude is shown; the
first time you told me of it it was almost the
first thing that you ever said to me.'

" 'So it was,' I answer quickly; 'and if the occasion were to come over again, I should say it again. I daresay you did not mean it, but it sounded exactly as if you were complaining of my father for being too careful of you.'

" 'He *is* too careful of me !' cries the young man, with a hot flushing of cheek and brow. 'I cannot help it if it make you angry again; I *must* say it, he is more careful of me than he would be of his own son, if he had one.'

" 'Did not he promise your mother that he would look after you ?' ask I eagerly. 'When people make promises to people on their death-beds they are in no hurry to break them; at least, such people as father are not.'

" 'You do not understand,' he says, a little impatiently, while that hot flush still dwells on his pale cheek; 'my mother was the last person in the world to wish him to take care of my body at the expense of my honour.'

"'What are you talking about?' I say, look-ing at him with a lurking suspicion that, de-spite the steady light of reason in his blue eyes, he is still labouring under some form of delirium.

"'Unless I tell you all my grievance, I see that you will never comprehend,' he says sigh-ing. 'Well, listen to me and you shall hear it, and if you do not agree with me, when I have done, you are not the kind of girl I take you for.'

"'Then I am sure I am not the kind of girl you take me for,' reply I, with a laugh; 'for I am fully determined to disagree with you en-tirely.'

"'You know,' he says, raising himself a little from his hay couch and speaking with clear rapidity, 'that whenever we take a French prize a lot of the French sailors are ironed, and the vessel is sent into port, in the charge of one officer and several men; there is

11

some slight risk attending it—for my part, I think *very* slight—but I suppose that your father looks at it differently, for—*I have never been sent.'*

" ' It is accident,' say I, reassuringly; 'your turn will come in good time.'

" ' It is *not* accident !' he answers, firmly. ' Boys younger than I am—much less trustworthy, and of whom he has not half the opinion that he has of me—have been sent, but *I, never*. I bore it as well as I could for a long time, but now I can bear it no longer; it is not, I assure you, my fancy; but I can see that my brother officers, knowing how partial your father is to me—what influence I have with him in many things—conclude that my not being sent is my own choice; in short, that I am—*afraid.'* (His voice sinks with a disgusted and shamed intonation at the last word.) 'Now—I have told you the sober facts—look me in the face' (putting his hand with boyish familiarity under my chin, and turning round my curls, my features, and the front view of my big comb towards him),. ' and tell me whether you agree with me, as I said you would, or not—whether it is not cruel kindness on his part to make me keep a whole skin on such terms ?'

" I look him in the face for a moment, trying to say that I do not agree with him, but it is more than I can manage. 'You were right,' I say, turning my head away, ' I *do* agree with you ; I wish to heaven that I could honestly say that I did not.'

" ' Since you do then,' he cries excitedly— ' Phœbe ! I knew you would, I knew you better than you knew yourself—I have a favour to ask of you, a *great* favour, and one that will keep me all my life in debt to you.'

" ' What is it ?' ask I, with a sinking heart.

" ' Your father is very fond of you——'

" ' I know it,' I answer curtly.

" 'Anything that you asked, and that was within the bounds of possibility, he would do,' he continues, with eager gravity. 'Well, this is what I ask of you : to write him a line, and let me take it, when I go, asking him to send me home in the next prize.'

"Silence for a moment, only the hay-makers laughing over their rakes. 'And if,' say I, with a trembling voice, 'you lose your life in this service, you will have to thank me for it; I shall have your death on my head all through my life.'

" 'The danger is infinitesimal, as I told you before,' he says, impatiently ; 'and even if it were greater than it is—well, life is a good thing, very good, but there are better things, and even if I come to grief, which is most un-likely, there are plenty of men as good as —better than—I, to step into my place.'

" 'It will be small consolation to the people who are fond of you that someone better than

you is alive, though you are dead,' I say, tearfully.

"'But I do not mean to be dead,' he says,
with a cheery laugh. 'Why are you so
determined on killing me? I mean to live
to be an admiral. Why should not I?'

"'Why indeed?' say I, with a feeble echo of
his cheerful mirth, and feeling rather ashamed
of my tears.

"'And meanwhile you will write?' he says,
with an eager return to the charge; 'and
soon? Do not look angry and pouting, as
you did just now, but I *must* go! What is
there to hinder me? I am getting up my
strength as fast as it is possible for any human
creature to do, and just think how I should
feel if they were to come in for something really
good while I am away.'

"So I wrote.

CHAPTER III.

" I OFTEN wished afterwards that my right
hand had been cut off before its fingers had
held the pen that wrote that letter. You
wonder to see me moved at what happened so
long ago—before your parents were born—and
certainly it makes not much difference now ;
for even if he had prospered then, and come
happily home to me, yet, in the course of
nature he would have gone long before now.
I should not have been so cruel as to have
wished him to have lasted to be as I am.
I did not mean to hint at the end of my story
before I have reached the middle. Well—and

so he went, with the letter in his pocket, and I felt something like the king in the tale, who sent a messenger with a letter, and wrote in the letter, 'Slay the bearer of this as soon as he arrives!' But before he went—the evening before, as we walked in the garden after supper, with our monstrously long shadows stretching before us in the moonlight—I do not think he said in so many words, 'Will you marry me?' but somehow, by some signs or words on both our parts, it became clear to us that, by-and-by, if God left him alive, and if the war ever came to an end, he and I should belong to one another. And so, having understood this, when he went he kissed me, as he had done when he came, only this time no one bade him; he did it of his own accord, and a hundred times instead of one; and for my part, this time, instead of standing passive like a log or a post, I kissed him back again, most lovingly, with many tears.

" Ah ! parting in those days, when the last
kiss to one's beloved ones was not unlikely to
be an adieu until the great Day of Judgment,
was a different thing to the listless, unemo-
tional good-byes of these stagnant times of
peace !

" And so Bobby also got into a post-chaise
and drove away, and we watched him too, till
he turned the corner out of our sight, as we
had watched father ; and then I hid my face
among the jessamine flowers that clothed the
wall of the house, and wept as one that would
not be comforted. However, one cannot weep
for ever, or, if one does, it makes one blind
and blear, and I did not wish Bobby to have a
wife with such defects ; so in process of time I
dried my tears.

" And the days passed by, and nature went
slowly and evenly through her lovely changes.
The hay was gathered in, and the fine new
grass and clover sprang up among the stalks

of the grass that had gone ; and the wild roses struggled into odorous bloom, and crowned the hedges, and then *their* time came, and they shook down their faint petals, and went.

"And now the corn harvest had come, and we had heard once or twice from our beloveds, but not often. And the sun still shone with broad power, and kept the rain in subjection. And all morning I sat at my big frame, and toiled on at the 'Last Supper.' I had finished Judas Iscariot's face and the other Apostles. I was engaged now upon the table-cloth, which was not interesting and required not much exercise of thought. And mother sat near me, either working too or reading a good book, and taking snuff—every lady snuffed in those days : at least in trifles, if not in great things, the world mends. And at night, when ten o'clock struck, I covered up my frame and stole listlessly upstairs to my room. There, I knelt at the open window, facing Plymouth and the sea, and asked God to take good care of father and Bobby. I do not know that I asked for any spiritual blessings for them, I only begged that they might be alive.

"One night, one hot night, having prayed even more heartily and tearfully than my wont for them both, I had lain down to sleep. The windows were left open, and the blinds up, that all possible air might reach me from the still and scented garden below. Thinking of Bobby, I had fallen asleep, and he is still mistily in my head, when I seem to wake. The room is full of clear light, but it is not morning : it is only the moon looking right in and flooding every object. I can see my own ghostly figure sitting up in bed, reflected in the looking-glass opposite. I listen : surely I heard some noise : yes—certainly, there can be no doubt of it—someone is knocking loudly and perseveringly at the hall-door. At first I fall into a deadly fear; then my reason comes to my aid. If it were a robber, or person with any evil intent, would he knock so openly and clamorously as to arouse the inmates ? Would not he rather go stealthily to work, to force a *silent* entrance for himself? At worst it is some drunken sailor from Plymouth ; at best, it is a messenger with news of our dear ones. At this thought I instantly spring out of bed, and hurrying on my stockings and shoes and whatever garments come most quickly to hand—with my hair spread all over my back, and utterly forgetful of my big comb, I open my door, and fly down the passages, into which the moon is looking with her ghostly smile, and down the broad and shallow stairs.

"As I near the hall-door I meet our old butler, also rather dishevelled, and evidently on the same errand as myself.

"'Who *can* it be, Stephens ?' I ask, trembling with excitement and fear.

" 'Indeed, ma'am, I cannot tell you,' replies the old man, shaking his head, 'it is a very odd time of night to choose for making such a noise. We will ask them their business, whoever they are, before we unchain the door.'

"It seems to me as if the endless bolts would never be drawn—the key never be turned in the stiff lock; but at last the door opens slowly and cautiously, only to the width of a few inches, as it is still confined by the strong chain. I peep out eagerly, expecting I know not what.

"Good heavens! What do I see? No drunken sailor, no messenger, but, oh joy! oh blessedness! my Bobby himself—my beautiful boy-lover! Even *now*, even after all these weary years, even after the long bitterness that followed, I cannot forget the unutterable happiness of that moment.

" 'Open the door, Stephens, quick!' I cry, stammering with eagerness. 'Draw the chain; it is Mr. Gerard; do not keep him waiting.'

" The chain rattles down, the door opens wide, and there he stands before me. At once, ere any one has said anything, ere anything has happened, a feeling of cold disappointment steals unaccountably over me—a nameless sensation, whose nearest kin is chilly awe. He makes no movement towards me ; he does not catch me in his arms, nor even 'hold out his right hand to me. He stands there still and silent, and though the night is dry, equally free from rain and dew, I see that he is dripping wet ; the water is running down from his clothes, from his drenched hair, and even from his eyelashes, on to the dry ground at his feet.

"' What has happened ?' I cry, hurriedly, ' How wet you are !' and as I speak I stretch out my hand and lay it on his coat sleeve. But even as I do it a sensation of intense cold runs up my fingers and my arm, even to the elbow. How is it that he is so chilled to the marrow of his bones on this sultry, breathless, August night? To my extreme surprise he does not answer; he still stands there, dumb and dripping. 'Where have you come from?' I ask, with that sense of awe deepening. 'Have you fallen into the river? How is it that you are so wet?'

"'It was cold,' he says, shivering, and speaking in a slow and strangely altered voice, 'bitter cold. I could not stay there.'

"'Stay where?' I say, looking in amazement at his face, which, whether owing to the ghastly effect of moonlight or not, seems to me ash white. 'Where have you been? What is it you are talking about?'

"But he does not reply.

"'He is really ill, I am afraid, Stephens,' I say, turning with a forlorn feeling towards the old butler. 'He does not seem to hear what I say to him.   I am afraid he has had a thorough chill.   What water can he have fallen into ? You had better help him up to bed, and get him warm between the blankets.   His room is quite ready for him, you know—come in,' I say, stretching out my hand to him, ' you will be better after a night's rest.'

" He does not take my offered hand, but he follows me across the threshold and across the hall.   I hear the water drops falling drip, drip, on the echoing stone floor as he passes; then upstairs, and along the gallery to the door of his room, where I leave him with Stephens. Then everything becomes blank and nil to me.

"I am awoke as usual in the morning by the entrance of my maid with hot water.

" ' Well, how is Mr. Gerard this morning ?' I ask, springing into a sitting posture.

"She puts down the hot water tin and stares at her leisure at me.

" ' My dear Miss Phœbe, how should *I*

know ?   Please God he is in good health and
safe, and that we shall have good news of him
before long.'

" ' Have not you asked how he is ?' I ask
impatiently.   ' He did not seem quite himself
last night; there was something odd about
him.   I was afraid he was in for another touch
of fever.'

" ' Last night—fever,' repeats she, slowly
and disconnectedly echoing some of my words.
' I beg your pardon, ma'am, I am sure, but I
have not the least idea in life what you are
talking about.'

" ' How stupid you are !' I say, quite at the
end of my patience.   ' Did not Mr. Gerard
come back unexpectedly last night, and did
not I hear him knocking, and run down to
open the door, and did not Stephens come too,
and afterwards take him up to bed ?'

" The stare of bewilderment gives way to a
laugh.

"'You have been dreaming, ma'am. Of course I cannot answer for what you did last night, but I am sure that Stephens knows no more of the young gentleman than I do, for only just now, at breakfast, he was saying that he thought it was about time for us to have some tidings of him and master.'

"'A dream!' cry I indignantly. 'Impossible! I was no more dreaming then than I am now.'

But time convinces me that I am mistaken, and that during all the time that I thought I was standing at the open hall-door, talking to my beloved, in reality I was lying on my bed in the depths of sleep, with no other company than the scent of the flowers and the light of the moon. At this discovery a great and terrible depression falls on me. I go to my mother to tell her of my vision, and at the end of my narrative I say,

"'Mother, I know well that Bobby is dead,

12

and that I shall never see him any more. I feel assured that he died last night, and that he came himself to tell me of his going. I am sure that there is nothing left for me now but to go too."

" I speak thus far with great calmness, but when I have done I break out into loud and violent weeping. Mother rebukes me gently, telling me that there is nothing more natural than that I should dream of a person who constantly occupies my waking thoughts, nor that, considering the gloomy nature of my apprehensions about him, my dream should be of a sad and ominous kind; but that, above all dreams and omens, God is good, that He has preserved him hitherto, and that, for her part, no devil-sent apparition shall shake her confidence in His continued clemency. I go away a little comforted, though not very much, and still every night I kneel at the open window facing Plymouth and the sea, and pray for my sailor boy. But it seems to me, despite all my self-reasonings, despite all that mother says, that my prayers for him are prayers for the dead.

CHAPTER IV.

" THREE more weeks pass away ; the harvest
is garnered, and the pears are growing soft and
mellow. Mother's and my outward life goes
on in its silent regularity, nor do we talk
much to each other of the tumult that rages
—of the heartache that burns, within each
of us. At the end of the three weeks, as we
are sitting as usual, quietly employed, and
buried each in our own thoughts, in the parlour, towards evening we hear wheels approaching the hall-door. We both run out
as in my dream I had run to the door, and
arrive in time to receive my father as he steps

out of the carriage that has brought him. Well! at least *one* of our wanderers has come home, but where is the other?

"Almost before he has heartily kissed us both—wife and child—father cries out, 'But where is Bobby?'

"'That is just what I was going to ask you,' replies mother quickly.

"'Is not he *here* with you?' returns he anxiously.

"'Not he,' answers mother, 'we have neither seen nor heard anything of him for more than six weeks.'

"'Great God!' exclaims he, while his face assumes an expression of the deepest concern, 'what *can* have become of him? what *can* have happened to the poor fellow?'

"'Has not he been with you, then?—has not he been in the *Thunderer?*' asks mother, running her words into one another in her eagerness to get them out.

"'I sent him home three weeks ago in a prize, with a letter to you, and told him to stay with you till I came home, and what can have become of him since, God only knows!' he answers with a look of the profoundest sorrow and anxiety.

"There is a moment of forlorn and dreary silence; then I speak. I have been standing dumbly by, listening, and my heart growing colder and colder at every dismal word.

"'It is all my doing!' I cry passionately, flinging myself down in an agony of tears on the straight-backed old settle in the hall. 'It is my fault—no one else's! The very last time that I saw him, I told him that he would have to thank me for his death, and he laughed at me, but it has come true. If I had not written *you*, father, that accursed letter, we should have had him here *now*, this *minute*, safe and sound, standing in the middle

of us—as we never, *never*, shall have him
again!'

"I stop, literally suffocated with emotion.

"Father comes over, and lays his kind
brown hand on my bent prone head. 'My
child,' he says, 'my dear child,' (and tears are
dimming the clear grey of his own eyes),
'you are wrong to make up your mind to
what is the worst at once. I do not disguise
from you that there is cause for grave anxiety
about the dear fellow, but still God is good;
He has kept both him and me hitherto; into
His hands we must trust our boy.'

"I sit up, and shake away my tears.

"'It is no use,' I say. 'Why should I
hope? There is no hope! I know it for a
certainty! He is *dead*' (looking round at
them both with a sort of calmness); 'he died
on the night that I had that dream—mother,
I told you so at the time. Oh, my Bobby!

I knew that you could not leave me for ever without coming to tell me !'

"And so speaking, I fall into strong hysterics and am carried upstairs to bed. And so three or four more lagging days crawl by, and still we hear nothing, and remain in the same state of doubt and uncertainty; which to me, however, is hardly uncertainty; so convinced am I, in my own mind, that my fair-haired lover is away in the land whence never letter or messenger comes—that he has reached the Great Silence. So I sit at my frame, working my heart's agony into the tapestry, and feebly trying to say to God that He has done well, but I cannot. On the contrary, it seems to me, as my life trails on through the mellow mist of the autumn mornings, through the shortened autumn evenings, that, whoever has done it, it is most evilly done. One night we are sitting round the little crackling wood fire that one does not

need for warmth, but that gives a cheerfulness
to the room and the furniture, when the butler
Stephens enters, and going over to father,
whispers to him. I seem to understand in
a moment what the purport of his whisper is.'

"'Why does he whisper?' I cry, irritably.
'Why does not he speak out loud? Why
should you try to keep it from me? I know
that it is something about Bobby.'

"Father has already risen, and is walking
towards the door.

"'I will not let you go until you tell me,'
I cry wildly, flying after him.

"'A sailor has come over from Plymouth,'
he answers hurriedly; 'he says he has news.
My darling, I will not keep you in suspense a moment longer than I can help, and
meanwhile pray — both of you pray for
him!'

"I sit rigidly still, with my cold hand

tightly clasped, during the moments that next elapse. Then father returns. His eyes are full of tears, and there is small need to ask for his message; it is most plainly written on his features—death, and not life.

" ' You were right, Phœbe,' he says, brokenly, taking hold of my icy hands; 'you knew best. He is gone! God has taken him.'

"My heart dies. I had thought that I had no hope, but I was wrong. 'I knew it!' I say, in a dry stiff voice. 'Did not I tell you so? But you would not believe me—go on! —tell me how it was—do not think I cannot bear it—make haste!'

"And so he tells me all that there is now left for me to know—after what manner, and on what day, my darling took his leave of this pretty and cruel world. He had had his wish, as I already knew, and had set off blithely home in the last prize they had captured. Father had taken the precaution of

having a larger proportion than usual of the
Frenchmen ironed, and had also sent a greater
number of Englishmen. But to what purpose? They were nearing port, sailing pros-
perously along on a smooth blue sea, with a
fair strong wind, thinking of no evil, when a
great and terrible misfortune overtook them.
Some of the Frenchmen who were not ironed
got the sailors below and drugged their grog;
ironed them, and freed their countrymen.
Then one of the officers rushed on deck, and
holding a pistol to my Bobby's head bade him
surrender the vessel or die. Need I tell you
which he chose? I think not—well" (with
a sigh) "and so they shot my boy—ah me!
how many years ago—and threw him overboard! Yes—threw him overboard—it makes
me angry and grieved even now to think of it
—into the great and greedy sea, and the vessel
escaped to France."

There is a silence between us: I will own

to you that I am crying, but the old lady's eyes are dry.

"Well," she says, after a pause, with a sort of triumph in her tone, "they never could say again that Bobby Gerard was *afraid !*

"The tears were running down my father's cheeks, as he told me," she resumes presently, "but at the end he wiped them and said, 'It is well! He was as pleasant in God's sight as he was in ours, and so He has taken him.'

"And for me, I was glad that he had gone to God—none gladder. But you will not wonder that, for myself, I was past speaking sorry. And so the years went by, and, as you know, I married Mr. Hamilton, and lived with him forty years, and was happy in the main, as happiness goes; and when he died I wept much and long, and so I did for each of my sons when in turn they went. But looking back on all my long life, the event

that I think stands out most clearly from it
is my dream and my boy-lover's death-day.
It *was* an odd dream, was not it?"

UNDER THE CLOAK.

UNDER THE CLOAK.

IF there is a thing in the world that my soul hateth, it is a long night journey by rail. In the old coaching days I do not think that I should have minded it, passing swiftly through a summer night on the top of a speedy coach with the star arch black-blue above one's head, the sweet smell of earth and her numberless flowers and grasses in one's nostrils, and the pleasant trot, trot, trot, trot, of the four strong horses in one's ears. But by railway! in a little stuffy compartment, with nothing to amuse you if you keep awake; with a dim lamp hanging above you, tan-

13

talizing you with the idea that you can read by its light, and when you try, satisfactorily proving to you that you cannot; and, if you sleep, breaking your neck, or at least stiffening it, by the brutal arrangement of the hard cushions.

These thoughts pass sulkily and rebelliously through my head as I sit in my salon, in the Ecu at Geneva, on the afternoon of the fine autumn day on which, in an evil hour, I have settled to take my place in the night train for Paris. I have put off going as long as I can. I like Geneva, and am leaving some pleasant and congenial friends, but now go I must. My husband is to meet me at the station in Paris at six o'clock to-morrow morning. Six o'clock! what a barbarous hour at which to arrive! I am putting on my bonnet and cloak; I look at myself in the glass with an air of anticipative disgust. Yes, I look trim and spruce enough now—a not disagreeable object perhaps—with sleek hair, quick and alert eyes, and pink-tinted cheeks. Alas! at six o'clock to-morrow morning, what a different tale there will be to tell! dishevelled, dusty locks, half-open weary eyes, a disordered dress, and a green-coloured countenance.

I turn away with a pettish gesture, and reflecting that at least there is no wisdom in living my miseries twice over, I go downstairs, and get into the hired open carriage which awaits me. My maid and man follow with the luggage. I give stricter injunctions than ordinary to my maid never for one moment to lose her hold of the dressing-case, which contains, as it happens, a great many more valuable jewels than people are wont to travel in foreign parts with, nor of a certain costly and beautiful Dresden china and gold Louis Quatorze clock, which I am carrying home as a present to my people. We

13—2

reach the station, and I straightway betake
myself to the first-class Salle d'Attente, there
to remain penned up till the officials undo the
gates of purgatory and release us—an arrangement whose wisdom I have yet to learn.
There are ten minutes to spare, and the salle
is filling fuller and fuller every moment.
Chiefly my countrymen, countrywomen, and
country children, beginning to troop home to
their partridges.   I look curiously round at
them, speculating as to which of them will be
my companion or companions through the
night.

There are no very unusual types : girls
in sailor hats and blonde hair-fringes ; strong-
minded old maids in painstakingly ugly
waterproofs ; baldish fathers ; fattish mothers ;
a German or two, with prominent pale eyes
and spectacles. I have just decided on the
companions I should prefer ; a large young
man, who belongs to nobody, and looks as if

he spent most of his life in laughing—(Alas! he
is not likely! he is sure to want to smoke!)—
and a handsome and prosperous-looking young
couple. They are more likely, as very probably,
in the man's case, the bride-love will overcome
the cigar-love. The porter comes up. The key
turns in the lock; the doors open. At first
I am standing close to them, flattening my
nose against the glass, and looking out on the
pavement; but as the passengers become more
numerous, I withdraw from my prominent
position, anticipating a rush for carriages. I
hate and dread exceedingly a crowd, and
would much prefer at any time to miss my
train rather than be squeezed and jostled by
one. In consequence, my maid and I are
almost the last people to emerge, and have
the last and worst choice of seats. We run
along the train looking in; the footman, my
maid, and I—full—full everywhere!

"Dames Seules?" asks the guard.

"Certainly not! neither 'Dames Seules,' nor 'Fumeurs,' but if it must be one or the other, certainly 'Fumeurs.'"

I am growing nervous, when I see the footman, who is a little ahead of us, standing with an open carriage door in his hand, and signing to us to make haste. Ah! it is all right! it always comes right when one does not fuss oneself.

"Plenty of room here, 'm; only two gentlemen!"

I put my foot on the high step and climb in. Rather uncivil of the two gentlemen! neither of them offers to help me, but they are not looking this way I suppose. "Mind the dressing-case!" I cry nervously, as I stretch out my hand to help the maid Watson up. The man pushes her from behind; in she comes—dressing-case, clock and all; here we are for the night!

I am so busy and amused looking out of the

window, seeing the different parties bidding their friends good-bye, and watching with indignation the barbaric and malicious manner in which the porters hurl the luckless luggage about, that we have steamed out of the station, and are fairly off for Paris, before I have the curiosity to glance at my fellow passengers. Well! when I do take a look at them, I do not make much of it. Watson and I occupy the two seats by one window, facing one another. Our fellow travellers have not taken the other two window seats; they occupy the middle ones, next us. They are both reading behind newspapers. Well! we shall not get much amusement out of them. I give them up as a bad job. Ah! if I could have had my wish, and had the laughing young man, and the pretty young couple, for company, the night would not perhaps have seemed so long. However I should have been mortified for them to have seen how *green* I looked when the dawn came; and, as to these commis voyageurs, I do not care if I look as green as grass in their eyes. Thus, all no doubt is for the best; and at all events it is a good trite copy-book maxim to say so. So I forget all about them: fix my eyes on the landscape racing by, and fall into a variety of thoughts. " Will my husband really get up in time to come and meet me at the station to-morrow morning? He does so cordially hate getting up. My only chance is his not having gone to bed at all! How will he be looking? I have not seen him for four months. Will he have succeeded in curbing his tendency to fat, during his Norway fishing? Probably not. Fishing, on the contrary, is rather a *fat-making* occupation; sluggish and sedentary. Shall we have a pleasant party at the house we are going to, for shooting? To whom in Paris shall I go for my gown? Worth? No, Worth is beyond me." Then I leave the future, and go back into past enjoyments; excursions to Lausanne; trips down the lake to Chillon; a hundred and one pleasantnesses. The time slips by: the afternoon is drawing towards evening; a beginning of dusk is coming over the landscape.

I look round. Good Heavens! what can those men find so interesting in the papers? I thought them hideously dull, when I looked over them this morning; and yet they are still persistently reading. What can they have got hold of? I cannot well see what the man beside me has; vis-à-vis is buried in an English *Times.* Just as I am thinking about him, he puts down his paper, and I see his face. Nothing very remarkable! a long black beard, and a hat tilted somewhat low over his forehead. I turn away my eyes hastily, for fear of being caught inquisitively scanning him; but still, out of their corners I see that he has taken a little bottle out of his travelling bag, has poured some of its contents into a glass, and is putting it to his lips. It appears as if—and, at the time it happens, I have no manner of doubt that he is drinking. Then I feel that he is addressing me. I look up and towards him : he is holding out the phial to me, and saying—

"May I take the liberty of offering Madame some ?"

"No thank you, Monsieur !" I answer, shaking my head hastily and speaking rather abruptly. There is nothing that I dislike more than being offered strange eatables or drinkables in a train, or a strange hymn book in church.

He smiles politely, and then adds—

"Perhaps the *other* lady might be persuaded to take a little."

"No thank you, sir, I'm much obliged to you," replies Watson briskly, in almost as ungrateful a tone as mine.

Again he smiles, bows, and re-buries himself in his newspaper. The thread of my thoughts is broken, I feel an odd curiosity as to the nature of the contents of that bottle. Certainly it is not sherry or spirit of any kind, for it has diffused no odour through the carriage. All this time the man beside me has said and done nothing. I wish he would move or speak, or do something. I peep covertly at him. Well! at all events, he is well defended against the night chill. What a voluminous cloak he is wrapped in; how entirely it shrouds his figure; trimmed with *fur* too! why it might be January instead of September. I do not know why, but that cloak makes me feel rather uncomfortable. I wish they would both move to the window, instead of sitting next us. Bah! am *I* setting up to be a timid dove? I, who rather pique myself on my bravery—on my indifference to tramps, bulls, ghosts? The clock has been deposited with the umbrellas, parasols, spare shawls, rugs, etc., in the netting above Watson's head. The dressing-case—a very large and heavy one—is sitting on her lap. I lean forwards and say to her—

"That box must rest very heavily on your knee, and I want a footstool—I should be more comfortable if I had one—let me put my feet on it."

I have an idea that, somehow, my sapphires will be safer if I have them where I can always feel that they are *there*. We make the desired change in our arrangements. Yes! both my feet are on it.

The landscape outside is darkening quickly now; our dim lamp is beginning to assert its importance. Still the men read. I feel a sensation of irritation. What can they mean by it? it is utterly impossible that they can decipher the small print of the *Times*, by this feeble shaky glimmer.

As I am so thinking, the one who had before spoken lays down his paper, folds it up and deposits it on the seat beside him. Then, drawing his little bottle out of his bag a second time, drinks, or seems to drink, from it. Then he again turns to me—

"Madame will pardon me, but if Madame *could* be induced to try a little of this; it is a cordial of a most refreshing and invigorating description; and if she will have the amiability to allow me to say so, Madame looks faint."

(What *can* he mean by his urgency? *Is* it pure politeness? I wish it were not growing so dark.) These thoughts run through my head as I hesitate for an instant what answer to make. Then an idea occurs to me, and I manufacture a civil smile and say, "Thank you very much, Monsieur! I am a little faint, as you observe. I think I will avail myself of your obliging offer." So saying, I take the glass, and touch it with my lips. I give you

my word of honour that I do not think I did
more; I did not mean to swallow a drop, but I
suppose I must have done. He smiles with a
gratified air.

"The other lady will now, perhaps, follow
your example ?"

By this time I am beginning to feel thoroughly uncomfortable: *why*, I should be
puzzled to explain. What *is* this cordial that
he is so eager to urge upon us ? Though determined not to subject *myself* to its influence,
I *must* see its effect upon another person.
Rather brutal of me, perhaps; rather in the
spirit of the anatomist, who, in the interest of
science, tortures live dogs and cats; but I am
telling you *facts*—not what I ought to have
done, but what I *did*. I make a sign to
Watson to drink some. She obeys, nothing
loath. She has been working hard all day ;
packing and getting under weigh, and she is
tired. There is no feigning about her ! She

has emptied the glass. Now to see what comes of it—what happens to my live dog! The bottle is replaced in the bag; still we are racing, racing on, past the hills and fields and villages. How indistinct they are all growing! I turn back from the contemplation of the outside view to the inside one. Why, the woman is asleep already! her chin buried in her chest; her mouth half open; looking exceedingly imbecile and very plain, as most people, when asleep out of bed, do look. A nice invigorating potion, indeed! I wish to Heaven that I had gone in Fumeurs, or even with that cavalcade of nursery-maids and unwholesome-looking babies in Dames Seules, next door. At all events, I am not at all sleepy myself: that is a blessing. I shall see what happens. Yes, by-the-by, I must see what he meant to happen: I must affect to fall asleep too. I close my eyes, and gradually sinking my chin on my chest, try to droop my jaws and hang my

cheeks, with a semblance of bonâ-fide slumber.
Apparently I succeed pretty well. After the
lapse of some minutes, I distinctly feel two
hands very cautiously and carefully lifting and
removing my feet from the dressing-box.

A cold chill creeps over me, and then the
blood rushes to my head and ears. What am
I to do? what am I to do? I have always
thought the better of myself ever since for it;
but, strange to say, I keep my presence of
mind. Still affecting to sleep, I give a sort of
kick, and instantly the hands are withdrawn
and all is perfectly quiet again. I now feign
to wake gradually, with a yawn and a stretch;
and, on moving about my feet a little, find that,
despite my kick, they have been too clever for
me, and have dexterously removed my box and
substituted another. The way in which I
make this pleasant discovery is that, whereas
mine was perfectly flat at the top, on the surface of the object that is now beneath my feet

there is some sort of excrescence—a handle of some sort or other. There is no denying it—brave I *may* be—I may laugh at people for running from bulls; for disliking to sleep in a room by themselves, for fear of ghosts; for hurrying past tramps: but now I am most thoroughly frightened. I look cautiously, in a sideways manner, at the man beside me. How very still he is! Were they *his* hands, or the hands of the man opposite him? I take a fuller look than I have yet ventured to do; turning slightly round for the purpose. He is still reading, or at least still holding the paper, for the reading must be a farce. I look at his hands: they are in precisely the same position as they were when I affected to go to sleep, although the pose of the rest of his body is slightly altered. Suddenly, I turn extremely cold, for it has dawned on me that they are not real hands—they are certainly false ones. Yes, though the carriage is shaking very much with

14

our rapid motion, and the light is shaking, too, yet there is no mistake. I look indeed more closely, so as to be quite sure. The one nearest me is ungloved; the other gloved. I look at the nearest one. Yes, it is of an opaque waxen whiteness. I can plainly see the rouge put under the finger-nails to represent the colouring of life. I try to give one glance at his face. The paper still partially hides it; and as he is leaning his head back against the cushion, where the light hardly penetrates, I am completely baffled in my efforts.

Great Heavens! what is going to happen to me? what shall I do? how much of him is *real?* where are his *real* hands? what is going on under that awful cloak? The fur border touches me as I sit by him. I draw convulsively and shrinkingly away, and try to squeeze myself up as close as possible to the window. But alas! to what good? how absolutely and utterly powerless I am! how entirely at their mercy! And there is Watson still sleeping swinishly! breathing heavily opposite me. Shall I try to wake her? But to what end? She, being under the influence of that vile drug, my efforts will certainly be useless, and will probably arouse the man to employ violence against me. Sooner or later in the course of the night I suppose they are pretty sure to murder me, but I had rather that it should be later than sooner.

While I think these things, I am lying back quite still, for, as I philosophically reflect, not all the screaming in the world will help me: if I had twenty-lung power I could not drown the rush of an express train. Oh, if my dear boy were but here,—my husband I mean,—fat or lean, how thankful I should be to see him! Oh, that cloak, and those horrid waxy hands! Of course I see it now! They remained stuck out, while the man's real ones were fumbling about my feet. In the

14—2

midst of my agony of fright, a thought of
Madame Tussaud flashes ludicrously across
me. Then they begin to talk of me. It is
plain that they are not taken in by my feint
of sleep : they speak in a clear, loud voice,
evidently for my benefit. One of them begins
by saying, " What a good-looking woman she
is—evidently in her première jeunesse too "—
(Reader, I struck thirty last May)—" and also
there can be no doubt as to her being of
exalted rank—a duchess probably."—(A dead
duchess by morning, think I grimly). They
go on to say how odd it is that people in my
class of life never travel with their own
jewels, but always with paste ones, the real
ones being meanwhile deposited at the bank-
ers. My poor, poor sapphires ! good-bye—
a long good-bye to you. But indeed I will
willingly compound for the loss of you and
the rest of my ornaments—will go bare-
necked, and bare-armed, or clad in Salviati

beads for the rest of my life, so that I do but attain the next stopping place alive.

As I am so thinking, one of the men looks, or I imagine that he looks, rather curiously towards me. In a paroxysm of fear lest they should read on my face the signs of the agony of terror I am enduring, I throw my pocket handkerchief—a very fine cambric one—over my face.

And now, oh reader, I am going to tell you something which I am sure you will not believe; I can hardly believe it myself, but, as I so lie, despite the tumult of my mind— despite the chilly terror which seems to be numbing my feelings—in the midst of it all a drowsiness keeps stealing over me. I am now convinced either that vile potion must have been of extraordinary strength, or that I, through the shaking of the carriage, or the unsteadiness of my hand, carried more to my mouth, and swallowed more—I did not *mean*

to swallow any—than I intended, for—you
will hardly credit it, but—I *fell asleep!*

* * * * *

* * * * *

When I awake,—awake with a bewildered
mixed sense of having been a long time asleep,
—of not knowing where I am—and of having
some great dread and horror on my mind—
awake and look round, the dawn is breaking.
I shiver, with the chilly sensation that the
coming of even a warm day brings, and look
round, still half unconsciously, in a misty way.
But what has happened ? how empty the carriage is ! the dressing-case is gone ! the clock
is gone ! the man who sat nearly opposite me
is gone ! *Watson is gone !* but the man in the
cloak and the wax hands still sits beside me !
Still the hands are holding the paper ; still the
fur is touching me ! Good God ! I am tête-à-
tête with him ! A feeling of the most appal-
ling desolation and despair comes over me—

vanquishes me utterly. I clasp my hands together frantically, and, still looking at the dim
form beside me, groan out—" Well! I did
not think that Watson would have forsaken
me!" Instantly, a sort of movement and
shiver runs through the figure: the newspaper drops from the hands, which however
continue to be still held out in the same position as if still grasping it; and behind the
newspaper, I see by the dim morning light
and the dim lamp-gleams that there is no real
face but a mask. A sort of choked sound is
coming from behind the mask. Shivers of
cold fear are running over me. Never to this
day shall I know what gave me the despair-
ing courage to do it, but before I know what
I am doing, I find myself tearing at the cloak,
—tearing away the mask—tearing away the
hands. It would be better to find *anything*
underneath—Satan himself,—a horrible dead
body — anything — sooner than submit any

longer to this hideous mystery. And I am rewarded. When the cloak lies at the bottom of the carriage—when the mask, and the false hands and false feet—(there are false *feet* too) —are also cast away, in different directions, what do you think I find underneath?

Watson! Yes: it appears that while I slept —I feel sure that they must have rubbed some more of the drug on my lips while I was un-conscious, or I never could have slept so heavily or so long—they dressed up Watson in the mask, feet, hands, and cloak; set the hat on her head, gagged her, and placed her beside me in the attitude occupied by the man. They had then, at the next station, got out, taking with them dressing-case and clock, and had made off in all security. When I arrive in Paris, you will not be surprised to hear that it does not once occur to me whether I am look-ing green or no.

And this is the true history of my night

journey to Paris! You will be glad, I dare say, to learn that I ultimately recovered my sapphires, and a good many of my other ornaments. The police being promptly set on, the robbers were, after much trouble and time, at length secured; and it turned out that the man in the cloak was an ex-valet of my husband's, who was acquainted with my bad habit of travelling in company with my trinkets— a bad habit which I have since seen fit to abandon.

What I have written is literally true, though it did not happen to myself.

THE END.

BILLING, PRINTER, GUILDFORD, SURREY.